D0481772

I AM THE ICE WORM

MARYANN EASLEY

BOYDS MILLS PRESS

Text copyright © 1996 by MaryAnn Easley

Special thanks to Jenna Kaufman.

Published by Caroline House
Boyds Mills Press, Inc.
A Highlights Company
815 Church Street
Honesdale, Pennsylvania 18431
Printed in the United States of America

Publisher Cataloging-in-Publication Data
Easley, MaryAnn.
    I am the ice worm / by MaryAnn Easley.—1st ed.
[128]p. : cm.
Summary : While traveling to visit her mother in the Arctic a California girl learns
the meaning of hardship and survival when she is taken in by an Inupiat family.
ISBN 1-56397-412-6
1. Inuit—Juvenile fiction. [1. Inuit—Fiction.] I. Title.
813.54—dc20   [F]   1996   CIP
Library of Congress Catalog Card Number 94-73318

First edition, 1996
Book designed by Abby Kagan
The text of this book is set in 12-point Goudy

10 9 8 7 6 5 4 3 2 1

For
Sherry and Tracy
with love;

And for the Iñupiat children
of the Northwest Arctic
who taught me
the meaning of survival.

1

FEBRUARY 1977

The coldest wind I'd ever felt in my life blasted me across the ice. Johnny Skye burst out laughing. He crossed his arms in front of his chest and laughed as if I were the biggest joke he'd ever seen.

"What's so funny?" I shouted.

He pointed to my feet and laughed and laughed. I'd slipped and fallen on the ice so many times that my luggage arrived in the little airport before I did. One of the Eskimos on my flight said to Johnny Skye, "She needs mukluks!," which sent him reeling with laughter again. I was a million miles from home. I wasn't in the mood to hear some bush pilot named Johnny Skye laughing at me.

"Your boots!" he said. "You've got to get rid of those 'lower 48' boots!"

My brand-new boots were white leather with pointed toes and rolled-down tops and fake silver spurs. They were the most expensive boots in the mall at South Coast Plaza, and probably the most popular boots in

Dana Point and Huntington Beach, and maybe even the whole state of California.

"Hey, kid, ain't you kind of gangly?" he said. "There's not enough meat on your bones to keep you warm 'round here. A stiff wind'll blow you right over."

"I want to call my mother," I said.

Johnny Skye laughed even more. There was ice on his wool scarf and ice on his yellow beard.

"Lots of luck, kid," he said. "They don't have phones up there, not where Linda Atwood is working. Didn't anyone tell you? This is *Alaska!*"

I glared at him, but he just grinned.

Johnny Skye was tall compared to the Eskimos, and he had straight, white teeth. He wore a black jumpsuit zipped to his chest and a tan parka with a furry hood. His boots were the biggest I'd ever seen, like big white bunny feet. Chunks of ice fell from them and melted into puddles on the dirty floor.

"No phones?" I asked.

"No phones, no electricity, and no plumbing where you're headed. That means no toilets either. Welcome to the Arctic!"

"You're joking! My mother would never come to a place that didn't have a phone."

"I'm dead serious," he said. He adjusted his cap and wiped the melting ice from his beard with a grimy mitten.

I sank onto one of the plastic chairs lining the wall. Only Mom would send someone like Johnny Skye to meet me. I hated her for leaving. I hated Dad for letting her go. I hated the year and a half since the bicentennial. That's when Dad and Mom had declared their independence from one another and from me. Now I was in Kotzebue, Alaska, and I couldn't have felt more miserable.

"Cheer up, kid," Johnny Skye said. He glanced at his watch as if he had an important appointment. "I've got some boots for you behind the counter over there, and there's a parka and a bedroll, too. The way you're built, you'll need all the goosedown you can get."

An Eskimo girl grinned from behind the airport counter. Her dark eyes were shaped like almonds. "Come! See!" she said, motioning with her hand. She wore a flowered top that wasn't a dress and wasn't a blouse either. It had a ruffle around the bottom and a hood at the collar.

Johnny Skye clutched the shoulder of my cream-colored cashmere coat and pulled me up from the chair. The girl held a huge, ugly parka and some fur-lined boots with soles at least three inches thick.

"Uh, no thanks," I said. "I've got my own clothes."

"Your mother told me what you needed," Johnny Skye said. "I bought everything over at Rotman's." He took the coat from the girl and held it out. "This here's got a wolverine ruff. That means it won't ice up."

"So?"

"Look here, young lady, there ain't no stores where you're headed. You're gonna have to sacrifice some of your stuck-up, fancy ideas."

Mom once had a whole closet full of clothes. I'd even

borrowed some of her stuff. She must have been out of her mind to ask Johnny Skye to shop for me.

He looked at his watch again. "Don't argue. Just put on the boots and dump what you need into that duffel bag. I'll bring along the rest of your gear next trip."

"Next trip! When will that be?"

"When we have better weather," he said.

"I need all my stuff," I said. "This is a major move, you know."

"It looks like you brought along everything you own," he said, opening some of my boxes and looking inside. "Come on, kid, put just your essentials in the bag. The plane's loaded. You want us to get off the ground, don't you?" He poked through my stuff, shaking his head and muttering to himself. I was sure he'd break something. "What are all these horse statues for?"

"I collect them."

I was ready to go back to Dad's place in Dana Point, even to his red Porsche and silly girlfriends.

"Do what Johnny Skye say," the Eskimo girl said. "Weather get worse maybe."

"That's right, kid," Johnny Skye said. "I'm making the run within ten minutes or I ain't going at all. The temperature's dropping, and we won't get over the pass. I'm the best damned bush pilot in the Northwest Arctic, but you better hustle or you ain't getting out of Kotzebue today, tomorrow, or the day after."

A lady at Alaska Airlines said I was lucky the flight to Kotzebue hadn't been cancelled. I'd hung around the Anchorage airport studying a stuffed grizzly in a glass case and flipping pages in magazines for three hours before the only plane scheduled for Kotzebue departed.

It had been a mistake to come. And the boots were too big.

"Put the socks on first," Johnny Skye said. He handed me a pair of thick thermal socks, then dug out a second pair from his pocket. "Always carry along extra. You never know when you might need them."

"They're so big and so . . . gray," I said.

"What did you expect?" he asked.

He waited until I put on the socks. The boots fit better.

I stuffed everything I could into the duffel. It swelled with my clothes, shampoo and conditioner, the teddy bear I'd had since I was three, my best jeans, favorite sweaters, and jewelry. I gave up my electric hair dryer and my portable television. Thank goodness I'd taken the trouble to put my posters into a long shipping tube, or they would have been crushed for sure! I found space for my tape player, even though I wasn't sure how long the batteries would last. I put in my journals and the new white boots Johnny Skye didn't like. I stuffed in my bicentennial cardigan sweater with the red, white, and blue stripes and '76 on the sleeve, and all my cassette tapes.

Johnny Skye took away my cashmere coat, saying it was too thin. He made me put on the horrible parka. Then he carried what was left of my stuff to a storage room behind the counter. I silently said good-bye to my horse collection and paperback novels, my photo albums and scrapbooks, my tennis racket, summer sandals, embroidered pillows and padded hangers, makeup mirror, manicure kit, bedspread, feather boa, and a ton of other things. I wanted to cry when I saw my boxes being carted away. They contained a part of home, a part of a time when we were a family in Huntington Beach. Inside were bits and pieces of me.

I followed Johnny Skye out the front door, through an enclosed porch, and out onto the dirty snow. I'd never been in such a place. Even in the middle of the day, it was as dark as night. There weren't any trees or sidewalks or billboard signs. Kotzebue didn't look like any place in Orange County, California. It was scary and unreal. Snarling dogs sat at the end of their chains on stained yellow snow. There weren't many lights, and it was quiet except for the howling of dogs and the sound of our footsteps squeaking in the snow.

Johnny Skye's plane was flimsy. A side window had been mended with silver duct tape. The seat on the passenger's side was split, and a spring was sticking out. I stood there staring at the spring.

"Better hop in back with the cargo," he said, shoving me aside. "It'll help balance my load."

I thought he was joking, but he waited while I climbed into the plane and crawled on my hands and knees to join the cargo. I wondered if Dad could get his money back, since I didn't actually have a seat.

Johnny Skye slammed the door, then came around and got into the pilot's seat. I peered out the side window. I couldn't believe I was leaving behind all my valuables just so Johnny Skye could haul out to nowhere crates of cigarettes, crackers, soft drinks, and stuff anyone could buy in any convenience store on just about any corner of the United States.

Once locked inside the crowded plane, I felt claustrophobic and a little panicky.

"Is it safe?" I shouted over the rattle of the engine. "Is the weather going to be okay? Do you have radar?" Johnny Skye was busy pulling switches and saying things into a microphone. He didn't answer.

Then he turned around and grinned. "Hang on, kid!"

Suddenly, the plane zigzagged across the ice. We weren't on a landing strip. We were on a frozen ocean! Ice flew past the windows. I could see aluminum boats along the shoreline, probably locked in ice since summer. I wondered if Johnny Skye had a license to pilot a plane. The engine coughed and sputtered. I crossed my fingers and shut my eyes, wishing with all my heart for home.

Then I felt the plane lift, dip, and lift again. We were off the ice and rising into the sky. Dogs chasing one another on the ice became smaller and smaller. The little spit of land disappeared below. Soon there was nothing to see out the tiny oval window but snow and ice.

2

THROUGH THE
LOOKING GLASS

The landscape below looked like the moon. There wasn't a single tree, not a building or a road, no sign of life at all.

I bounced on cargo wedged into the plane—duffel bags, sacks of rice, potatoes, flour, crates of canned milk, cases of Pilot Boy bread, soft drinks, cigarettes, and cardboard boxes tied with string.

I leaned against my bedroll. There were butterflies in my stomach. I kept telling myself this was an adventure, that I could write about the experience when I was a world-famous author. Frankly, I was scared to death.

"Where are we going?" I shouted.

"You couldn't pronounce it if I told you, kid," Johnny Skye shouted back.

Mom had given my destination to a careless stranger, but not to me. I was fourteen, but she still didn't believe I was old enough to take care of myself.

Someone had to rescue Mom. She sure didn't belong in Alaska.

"Your mother's so cavalier," Dad had said. "She tells us nothing—'Buy a ticket to Kotzebue via Anchorage. Johnny Skye will meet you and fly you to the village.' " Dad looked me in the eyes. "Are you sure you want to go?"

I wasn't sure at all. "What else did she say?" I asked.

"Only 'Holy snowballs, it's cold in February! Dress accordingly.' " Dad flung the letter, his jaws clenched. He tossed down his charge card. "Get what you need."

"What about school?" I asked.

"She'll homeschool you, I suppose," he said. As usual, he was deciding my fate. "After all, she's a teacher."

Mom had left to find herself. She needed a job, and there weren't any in California. By the time she started looking out of state, Dad and I had moved to Dana Point. At least I was still close to home because Dana Point was only forty-five minutes from where we used to live in Huntington Beach.

Now my destiny was in the hands of a lunatic bush pilot with duct tape on his windows. I studied the cases of cola under my feet and huddled inside my parka. The wolverine ruff felt warm against my face. I tried to think of flying to Hawaii or Tahoe or places we'd been together as a family. My mind filled with memories of days around our swimming pool and on our sailboat. I tried to concentrate on anything except where I was at the moment.

I knew enough to figure out Johnny Skye's plane had only a single engine and practically no equipment. The plane rattled and shook as it bounced in the air. I listened to the straining engine, and thought of Dad and his flying lessons. He'd gotten his pilot's license, but he gave up flying after a trip to Catalina when he made a bad landing and damaged the wheel of a rented plane. He took a commercial jet home, and that was the end of his career as a pilot.

He blamed it on Mom. He said she'd never shown any interest in his flying. Mom was claustrophobic like me. She got panicky in small, cramped places. Dad said she ought to grow up sometime. He never understood Mom. Just like he never understood me. Well, I understood. And I was going to bring her back home. Maybe Dad would change if we all got together again.

"Can't we go higher?" I shouted.

"Wings will ice up," Johnny Skye shouted back.

We continued along a pass with mountains on either side. They glistened, gigantic and white, beneath a monstrous moon.

I had no idea how long we'd been flying or how far we were going. Temperatures could drop as low as 70 degrees below zero because of the wind-chill factor. I didn't know exactly how wind chill worked, but my favorite climate was about 72 degrees *above* zero.

Whether I got to Mom or not depended entirely on Johnny Skye, a hot shot pilot who didn't take very good care of his plane.

"We're flying awfully low, aren't we?" I shouted.

The engine coughed. Johnny Skye flipped switches. There was a gasp, then a gulping sound.

"Do we have enough fuel? I mean, that was pretty

close, wasn't it?" Johnny Skye didn't answer. A mountain loomed ahead. "Look out!" I shouted.

Johnny Skye pulled up the nose of the plane just in time. We soared into the crystal-clear night where a galaxy of stars whirled around us. I was scared to death, but he had no fear. He turned around and grinned. "No problem, hon," he said. "I can handle it."

"Maybe we should turn back and wait for daylight," I said. I crossed my fingers and wished on all the stars that Johnny Skye would do just that.

"No way!" he shouted. "If we go back, it'll mean waiting a week or longer. In this business, you have to take risks. You're flying with Johnny Skye, honey, and Johnny Skye ain't worried about a little bit of weather."

We rose higher, but the pass kept rising, too. We hovered close to the ground even though we were steadily climbing. Then Johnny Skye turned around in his seat, and this time he wasn't grinning. He was squinting, trying to see the wing through a side window.

He swore and hit the control panel with a fist. "Damn! Wings are icing up!"

The butterflies rose from my stomach to my throat. I waited, hugging my bedroll. I told myself Johnny Skye was probably the kind of guy who liked scaring people, especially girls.

It was like descending in a fast elevator. The ground swelled below. The engine groaned. Any second I thought he'd pull us out of the dive. Johnny Skye tried to bring up the nose, but the plane dropped even lower.

"Uh-oh!" he said.

The engine coughed, then died. Utter silence. Only the sound of my heart. We fell through the darkness, descending down, down, too fast. I shut my eyes and waited for the crash. I waited to die.

Then I had the oddest memory. I remembered when I was little and walking between Mom and Dad. Mom held my left hand. Dad held my right. When we came to a curb, they lifted me high in the air, swinging me across onto the sidewalk. It was a game we played. That was when Dad was just starting out as a lawyer and Mom wore long dresses and flowers in her hair.

"Wheee!" Mom would squeal, making me soar like an airplane above the ground.

"Look at Allison," Dad would say. "Coming in for a landing! Look out!"

I didn't look. The plane shuddered as if coming apart. I was only fourteen. I was too young to die.

There was the sound of metal scraping ice. The plane bounced up and down like a toy, then coasted as if it might take off again. I opened my eyes. Wooden boxes were falling like blocks. Packages split open. Cartons hurtled past me. I held on to my bedroll as if it were a life preserver. I could hardly breathe. My legs were twisted and cramped. I thought the plane would bounce and skid forever. Then something caught. The plane jerked, spun around, and slammed into a bluff of snow. Suddenly there was blackness and silence.

Someone was moaning. It was me. I pushed my heavy duffel out of the way. Then I struggled to sit up and free my legs. What a mess! It was as if someone had dumped the contents of a small store around me. There were clothes and food and cartons of cigarettes and candy bars.

"Johnny Skye!" I shouted. "Hey, we made it!"

My voice was high and strange. My chest hurt as if it had been hit with a baseball bat. But I was alive! Johnny Skye had managed to get the plane down in one piece!

"Mr. Skye?"

He didn't make a sound. The oval window was broken, and beyond it was a wall of white. I poked a finger into the crack and touched the snow. It spilled inside like sugar.

"Guess we'll have to hike," I said. There was no answer. "Johnny Skye? What's the matter?" It took every ounce of strength to call his name again. "Hey, Johnny Skye! Are you all right?"

3

INTO A LAND OF WONDER

I crawled forward to the cockpit. Johnny Skye was slumped over the controls. "Hey, wake up!" I shouted, touching him on the shoulder.

There was a big gash on his head. He didn't open his eyes. He didn't move or make a sound.

"Wake up! Please wake up!" I said, shaking him. My breath steamed in front of my face, then fell like dew on my scarf. Within seconds, ice had formed where the dew had fallen.

"It's freezing," I said. The duct tape on the side window was broken. "We've got to keep warm. Are you okay?"

Johnny Skye looked odd and strangely waxen.

I quickly took my hand away. I'd never seen a dead person in my whole life. It was a nightmare, the most terrible nightmare I could imagine, but this wasn't a dream.

"No, no, no!" I screamed. "You can't do this to me! You can't just die!"

I decided to cover him up. I dug through the cargo

with stiff, awkward fingers until I found a canvas tarp. I threw it over him without touching him.

"Stay calm," I said to myself. "Don't panic. Do something."

I picked up the radio mike and pushed the button. "Hello, hello! Is anyone there?"

There was no answer. Not even static. The radio was dead.

I hit the mike against the cockpit dash and tried again. No luck.

"Keep warm," I said, shivering. "Keep warm."

I crawled out of the cockpit, carefully avoiding the canvas mound in the pilot's seat.

If the plane was going to blow up, I figured it would have already done so. I decided it was best to wait for help to come the way Mom waited along the freeway when a tire blew. I needed to stay warm. I pulled clothes out of my duffel and put on an extra sweater and a second pair of socks. I found the thick padded coveralls left over from the time we'd gone skiing at Tahoe. I didn't want to bring them. They were out of style, but Dad insisted I might need them. I yanked a big woolen cap down low over my ears and pulled up my parka hood. The wolverine ruff that Johnny Skye promised wouldn't ice up encircled my face. Then I climbed inside my bedroll.

"Someone will come to take me home," I said, but there was no one around to hear.

I rocked back and forth, holding myself and moaning. Gradually, I got warmer. The cold left my fingers and toes, but my nose stayed numb. I was used to waiting.

Wasn't I always waiting for Dad? He'd forgotten to pick me up more times than I could count. He just wasn't dependable that way. I'd have to take the bus or get a ride with a friend at the last minute, but Dad would always have a good excuse. A jury trial lasted longer than he'd expected, or a client completely broke down in his office, or he'd won the tennis tournament or the yacht race or the waterskiing trophy and couldn't leave the big celebration afterward.

Mom never forgot to pick me up, but she'd been gone for months. I could only depend on myself. I always had a backup plan when I went anywhere or did anything. I had friends or bus money or walked. Well, I had no backup plan for a plane crash.

I finally stopped shivering and escaped into sleep.

"Oh, Allison, I feel so fragmented," Mom had said. "Why can't people live in harmony with nature and each other. We're outlaws, you know, polluting the rivers and streams, scarring the mountains, spoiling our oceans. It's part of the human condition."

I awoke with a start, expecting Mom to be there, but I was still very much alone. I rolled down my mitten cuff to look at my watch, the watch Dad had given me for Christmas. Three o'clock. I had no idea if it was three o'clock in the afternoon or three o'clock in the morning.

I listened and waited, thinking surely Mom would send someone to rescue me. She'd be worried by now. Once Dad knew, he'd make some calls. He knew the right people. He had contacts.

I remembered how eager Dad had been to get me on the plane because he was already late for a date.

"I wouldn't allow you to go off on your own if I had any question about this," he said. "And it seems your mother has it all arranged. This Johnny Skye will take care of everything, and you've got my charge card and the phone card, too. Call when you get there and let me know you arrived safely." He waved good-bye, then added, "And say hello to Mom. Tell her . . . well, tell her hello."

I cried until there were no tears left. I was all alone in the wilderness with a dead man.

Through a window, I could see snow blowing like veils and drifting into steep piles around the plane. The thought of being buried alive made me move from my warm cocoon and crawl up to the cockpit door. Snow was piling high. It looked like whipped cream, soft and white, but it would eventually cover the plane. Who could find me then?

I pulled on the door handle, but it wouldn't budge. I tried again. The door seemed welded shut. I was trapped inside. I banged on the handle with my fists. There was a brittle, cracking sound. The door unlatched, but it still wouldn't open. I leaned back and pushed with my feet. I kicked as hard as I could. "Help! Help!" I shouted until I had no breath left.

When I got the door open a crack, a shock of freezing cold air swept inside.

How stupid! It had been a crazy idea to open the door. I quickly yanked it shut. In only a few seconds, the cockpit was freezing.

I'd read about a thirteen-year-old boy who'd been marooned on an ice floe caught in an outgoing tide. He was rescued by helicopter after spending over an hour on the drifting ice. He had hypothermia and frostbitten heels. I wrote about it in my journal and wondered what I would do in a situation like that, drifting all alone on a chunk of ice waiting for someone to rescue me.

I tried to stay calm, to not think about being inside such a tiny plane. My heart was racing. I was breathing too fast.

At home, I'd know just what to do, but there were no emergency call boxes here I could walk to, no patrol cars cruising by, nothing but snow and ice. I listened, waiting to hear a search plane overhead. I listened, but no one came.

"Please, please, please God," I said, shutting my eyes tightly and pleading to anyone who might listen. "I want to go *home*."

When I opened my eyes, I saw something move outside the front window of the plane. It looked like a grizzly bear, big and furry.

It was a man, dressed in fur from head to toe, and not like any I'd seen before. He was an Eskimo, but more primitive looking than the Eskimos I'd seen in Kotzebue. He banged on the cockpit door, shouting something in a foreign language.

He tugged on the door, grunting. I cowered inside, scared to death. Then I realized he'd come to rescue me. I started pushing and kicking the door from inside. When the door finally opened, the man held out a hand that was bare and warm. A team of dogs waited in front of a long wooden sled, their tongues hanging out as they stretched on their lines.

"Did my mom send you? Thank goodness, you found

me!" My teeth were chattering. "We crashed. I don't know how long we've been here. Johnny Skye's dead!" I started to cry. I was happy and sad and scared all at the same time.

The man just stared at me. It was a miracle he'd found me at all! Wind had whipped the snow into drifts around the plane and it was nearly buried.

The man's eyes were almond-shaped, and his face, partly hidden by the fur of his parka hood, was as brown as a walnut. He must have been old because some of his front teeth were missing.

He climbed inside the plane. When he came out, he was shaking his head, even though I'd already told him Johnny Skye was dead. I stuck my hands deep into the pockets of my parka and felt the extra pair of socks that Johnny had given me. Death was so final, so absolute. Without good-byes.

The old man looked at me closely. "*Kiña atqin?*"

I shrugged, not understanding.

"*Kiña atqin?*" he asked again.

He pointed at me. I thought he wanted to know if he'd rescued the right person.

"Yes, it's me, Allison Atwood from California. Did my dad call you?"

He grinned. "Ah, Al . . . eee," he said mispronouncing my name. Then he pointed to himself. "Ikayauq," he said. It was a harsh-sounding name. "Come!" He motioned for me to follow him to the sled.

"Wait, I have to get my stuff. And what about Johnny Skye? We can't just leave him out here in the snow."

He frowned while we played a game of charades once again. He pointed to his loaded sled.

"You'll call someone, won't you? You'll make sure someone comes and takes care of things. I mean, what about Johnny Skye?"

He just grinned. I don't think he understood a word I said. He carried my duffel and bedroll—all that he would allow—to the sled. I sat on top of them in the rear, and he threw a big fur skin over my lap. It had a strong, repulsive odor, but it was warm. Beyond my feet, a large dead animal lay across the wooden slats. I couldn't see the animal's face, only its back. The fur stood out stiffly, and there was frozen blood on the sled railings. There were some smaller animals in a pile at the front of the sled, and they were almost covered with the falling snow.

"Wolverine," Ikayauq said, pointing out the largest animal with the feathery tail. He motioned to the smaller animals. "Muskrat. Fox."

He seemed really proud of himself to have those horrible dead animals on his sled. The huskies waited, their tails curled and switching. Some of them turned around and snarled. Some pawed the icy air. Others stood still as statues, staring off into the distance.

Nothing looked very clean on the sled. Everything was coated with grease.

Ikayauq stepped up on a little runner in back and the slats creaked with his weight. He shouted something to the dogs, and they shot forward, yelping with excitement as they strained on their harnesses. They ran lightly over the snow, pulling the sled, Ikayauq, and me—the whoosh of the sled runners the only sound.

Ikayauq's sled looked old-fashioned. It was made out of wood, but it was sturdy and held a lot of weight. The runners were covered with strips of bone or antler, and leather strings were wrapped around the slats. The slats twisted and strained and squeaked. I thought they would break as we raced over snowdrifts and across frozen lakes and ponds.

As far as I could see there was nothing but white snow and black sky. I wondered how Ikayauq knew the way. There were no trail markers or signs, nothing to give us directions. Overhead were a zillion stars and a swirling greenish veil of light that looked like something on another planet.

I had this creepy feeling I was somewhere outside myself, watching. Nothing was real or familiar, not Ikayauq or the huskies or the stark, white land. I felt like a space traveler as I soared along. My cheeks were stinging, and my woolen scarf was covered with crystals of ice. I was lucky to be alive, lucky to have Ikayauq's smelly fur blanket to protect me from the gusts of wind that dusted me with snow. I was the luckiest, most terrified girl in the world. I couldn't keep my teeth from chattering. I couldn't keep from shivering or smiling. It was only a matter of time and I'd be with Mom. I was rescued!

Ikayauq drove his huskies, never stopping, never looking back, going only forward, on and on.

I thought Ikayauq would never stop. There was no sign of life anywhere, only ice and snow.

4

LOST

I was freezing. There was no feeling in my hands and feet. My nose was numb in spite of the wolverine ruff and the heavy woolen scarf across my face. We finally stopped near a steep snowdrift. The dogs yelped and jumped, their tongues hanging out, steam rising from their mouths.

The first thing Ikayauq did was toss fish to the dogs. There was a stack of frozen fish on the sled, and he pulled them out one at a time and threw them into the air. The pack of dogs went wild, fighting over each fish, snarling and snapping their jaws. Then they settled down on the snow, their sharp teeth gnawing noisily on the rock-hard fish.

Ikayauq pulled out a long knife and started cutting out big blocks of snow. Within an hour, he had built a real igloo. It was small, about the size of a large doghouse. The wind was howling and scooping up sheets of snow. He took some animal skins inside, then stuck his head out the opening and motioned for me to enter. I didn't exactly trust him; he was old and only spoke a few words of English. Still, it was a relief to crawl inside the shelter away from the freezing wind.

"Caribou," he said, pointing to where I should sit on the pile of skins. He watched me closely as if expecting me to give him a compliment.

"Uh, very nice," I said. "Can we build a fire?" Ikayauq didn't understand. He grinned and nodded while I pulled off my mittens with my teeth. My hands felt dead. I held them close to the oil lamp, and my fingers began to sting. It felt as if my hands were being stuck with a million sharp needles. They were as red as strawberries. It took a long time for the stinging to stop.

Ikayauq didn't seem to notice how miserable I was. He lay on the caribou skins, smacking his lips and licking his fingers as he chewed on a ragged piece of fish. His chin went round and round as he chewed. He had no manners. He dipped a chunk into a cup of bad-smelling oil and held it toward me. The grease dripped from his fingers.

I shook my head. "Uh, no thanks."

With his hood pulled back, I could see his gray hair and smooth face. Even though he had teeth missing, he still grinned a lot, and in spite of being old and bow-legged, he was agile. It didn't matter one bit to him if he had to squat on his heels or move around on his hands and knees in the tiny, cramped igloo.

After he ate the fish, he crawled outside. I suppose he went out to check the dogs. He'd unharnessed them and chained them to stakes. He treated them more like servants than pets, bossing them around and hitting them if they didn't obey.

The igloo grew warm and cozy. I became so drowsy I let my guard down for a minute, sank into the smelly caribou skins, and fell asleep.

I dreamt of home. It was my thirteenth birthday, and Mom and Dad were getting divorced. In my dream, I remembered how happy but sad it was to be turning thirteen while my family was breaking up. Mom was gone the next day, and there was a "For Sale" sign on our house. Before I knew it, Dad and I were in Dana Point. I had to remind him when my fourteenth birthday came around, and he never once asked if I liked living in Dana Point.

When I woke up, Ikayauq was relighting the lamp. I could tell from the steam that came from his breath that he'd been outside. He'd gotten more frozen fish from his sled. He placed a piece over the lamp to thaw. Then he crawled out and the dogs started yelping like crazy.

"Al . . . eee!" he shouted from outside. "Al . . . eee! Al . . . eee!"

I thought he'd gotten hurt or something. Then I realized he was calling me. I crawled to the entrance and peered outside. It was dark, but the wind had stopped, and snow had settled into creamy sculptures around our camp.

Ikayauq expected me to help with the dogs, but I kept a safe distance. Those dogs were vicious. They weren't the kind of dogs you pet. They snarled and showed their fangs. They seemed ready to chomp on any arm or leg that got in the way. Ikayauq had to hold each dog in place, his arms around its neck, its wiggling body between his knees, while he locked the harness. He was grumbling, maybe even swearing, in his strange language. I stood shivering like crazy, my hands and feet getting numb.

Ikayauq repacked the sled. When he was ready to go, I started to climb on top. He grabbed me by the arm and pulled me off. Then he let me know by signaling with his hands and demonstrating with his feet that I was going to walk. His words sounded harsh, but he spoke in low, hushed tones and he didn't look angry. I guess he thought I needed some exercise.

Well, the creaky old sled wasn't that comfortable anyway. I dug my mittens out of my pockets and yanked them on. Then I pulled up my parka hood, drew the ruff low, and wrapped the woolen scarf across my face. Ikayauq stepped up on the sled runner, shouted to the dogs, and in a flash he was gone.

I followed, my boots grinding into the snow and making squeaky, crunchy sounds. Every step was an effort. It was like walking on packing foam. I hurried as fast as I could, following the sound of the yelping dogs. My heart pounded like a tom-tom. The old man was leaving me behind in a land without end. There was nothing as far as I could see.

I followed Ikayauq's trail in the snow. The sound of my grinding footsteps echoed around me. I was as alone as an astronaut walking on the moon.

"Ikayauq!" I shouted. My voice rose into the blue-black sky above an immense white planet of ice. There was no sign of life. "Ikayauq! Come back!"

I hurried along the indentations made by the sled runners and the scattered paw prints of the dogs. My breath burned in my throat. Tears froze on my eyelashes. Ikayauq had seemed like a nice old man, but he'd left me completely stranded. Like Johnny Skye. Like Mom. Like Dad.

I dug my heels into the crunchy snow and cursed Ikayauq. I tripped, falling into a drift without shadow, a ridge impossible to see. The snow was so dry and powdery that it spilled easily from my parka as I got to my feet. I struggled through piles of snow, my boots twisting and turning and sinking.

Then the sounds of the dogs came closer. Ikayauq had returned! The sled circled around me and stopped. "Al . . . eee!" Ikayauq shouted, grinning. "Feet warm now? Al . . . eee can ride."

I stomped over to the greasy sled without a word and climbed on with the dead animals and smelly skins.

I folded my arms in front of me and clenched my jaws. It was Mom's fault I was above the Arctic Circle. She should never have come.

"I can make it on my own," she said. "I have a teaching credential. Surely there's a job someplace, maybe at a rural school out in the country."

Dad, of course, laughed. Mom had never lived anywhere but the city. She hated the time we'd gone camping. "You like your creature comforts," he said. How could she get along without her weekly housekeeper? How could she cope without going to the hairdresser or having her nails done?

"I haven't always been so artificial," she said.

30

I pictured Mom writing poetry and wearing flowers, her eyes outlined in black, her lips pale, her hair hanging to her shoulders. That's how she looked in my albums, the photos taken of her at Berkeley, before Mom gave up trying to change the world, and changed herself instead.

Something gleamed in the distance. I kept my eyes on the horizon, but only a few dilapidated structures came into view. There was a flash of silver. It was an aluminum wall.

I imagined how it would be to sit inside Mom's house and be warm and comfortable. We could stay awhile, and I'd write everything in my journal. Then we'd go back to our real home, back to where we belonged, back to Dad.

As we drew closer, I could see a few huts clustered together, their rooftops covered with snow. The place looked abandoned and forgotten. Did people actually live in such an isolated place?

The dogs pulled close to a hut where other dogs paced back and forth, their long chains stretching from stakes driven into the snow. Ikayauq shouted a greeting, and children came to doorways of the huts, laughing and squealing. Women stood together, chattering as they stared at me. I searched the faces for Mom, but she wasn't there.

"Where's my mother?" I asked. "Where's Mrs. Atwood?"

A child pointed at me as she wrinkled her nose. Another laughed. Ikayauq began unloading the sled.

"My mother," I said. "I must find my mother."

Ikayauq glanced at the others, then scratched his ear.

"My mother," I said, speaking louder so he'd understand. "You know, she's the teacher. Her name's Linda Atwood. Where's the school?"

Ikayauq grinned. "School?" he said. "No school."

My heart sank. Ikayauq hadn't brought me home at all. I was lost in the Arctic.

5

NALUAGMI

The Eskimos came out of their huts to see Ikayauq as if he were a big hero. Their houses were no more than shacks constructed of wood or pieces of sheet metal. One was sort of dug out of the earth like a mole hill. Frozen fish were stacked like firewood against each sidewall. An old snowmobile, oil drums, cardboard boxes, cans, animal antlers, and things you'd normally throw away were heaped in piles. The snow had almost covered the junk.

Boys hurried to release Ikayauq's dogs, quickly chaining them to metal stakes. Girls tossed frozen fish to the snarling pack. Ikayauq picked up the dead wolverine and carried it to his shack. It was so heavy he wobbled as he walked. He hung it upside down in a little enclosed porch.

I stood by myself, feeling out of place and embarrassed because of their watching eyes. I kept expecting to see Mom. I waited, but she never appeared.

Ikayauq's hut looked unfinished. It wasn't painted, and

the insulation was exposed in places. The outside wooden door was nearly black with grease and fingerprints.

I'd never known anyone so poor. Ikayauq pulled open the door and welcomed everyone inside to see the dead animals on his floor. I followed him through the porch. Some of the animals had been placed there in a pile.

The inside door was in worse condition because it was split in places. I dawdled, thinking I'd better go back outside, but Ikayauq motioned with his hands and insisted I follow.

When I entered, I could smell animal skins and cooking fat. The room was stuffy, and there weren't any chairs. Everyone sat on the floor.

Before I knew it, I was surrounded by almond-eyed, black-haired strangers who stared at me and whispered behind their hands. Naked babies were tossed in the air and jiggled on hips and passed from one person to another. A woman was sewing something out of an animal hide. She put the stiff piece of hide into her mouth and chewed on it. Then she stitched some more. Her upper front teeth were worn to the gums.

"Al . . . eee," Ikayauq said, introducing me to everyone with a grin. He sang out my name as if calling from far away.

It was a relief to be safe inside, but I couldn't understand why Ikayauq had brought me here. I stood, wringing my hands. How would my mother ever find me? I should have stayed with the plane.

"I must find my mother," I said. "She'll be terribly worried about me by now."

Ikayauq chattered away, pointing at me as he explained to everyone how he'd found me. They looked at me as if I'd just come from Mars. I sat on the floor. I could see it would be awhile before we'd be on our way.

A woman stood beside an oil stove, cutting up meat and dropping small pieces into a steaming pot. Soon she brought me a bowl of thin soup. I dipped a bent spoon into the bowl, and tiny bits of meat spun through the sparse amount of rice.

"*Tuttu*," a little girl said, pointing to the soup.

It didn't look like any soup I'd seen before, but it smelled all right.

"Caribou," Ikayauq said, licking his lips as he dished up some for himself.

The woman giggled and put a hand over her mouth. She bent over, feet spread apart, to adjust her flowered parka dress. A baby squirmed inside the loose hood. Until that moment, I had no idea there was a baby sleeping on her back.

There were too many people for such a small space. Everyone sat closely together. Kids climbed over adults, wrestling with one another. No one scolded them or told them to sit still. Every time a baby cried, someone picked it up and tickled or teased it until it laughed. Everyone seemed happy and contented. After a while, Ikayauq fell asleep on the floor, a child dozing on his chest.

Some men brought in a few of the dead animals and dumped them on the floor. They cut them open right there in the house. My stomach rolled, and I thought I might throw up the soup I'd just eaten. Women scraped the animal skins with sharp round blades. It was a repulsive sight, but no one seemed to think it was anything out of the ordinary.

The room became hot with all the people inside and the oil stove roaring away. The hotter it got, the worse it smelled, like sweat and urine, dead animals and rotten food. I peeled off my cap and mittens and parka.

A girl popped corn at the stove, and the children ate it as fast as it was ready, spilling kernels all over the floor.

The Eskimos talked quietly as they worked on the animals. They laughed a lot, as if they were really enjoying themselves. I listened to their strange language and felt closed off from them, an intruder.

"May I use the bathroom?" I asked. Everyone stared at me. "Toilet?" I asked.

A woman put a hand over her mouth and laughed until she cried. "Toilet freeze bottom maybe," she said.

She motioned outside, and I thought they might have a portable toilet or something. No such luck! I could hear a woman laughing as I squatted behind the oil cans. I didn't waste any time because it was so cold and dark. For Ikayauq's family, it was camping out forever—with no toilets, not even an outhouse, and no showers or televisions or radios, nothing but snow and ice.

After a while, the smell in the house wasn't so bad, and it was comfortable and warm. I got drowsy and fell asleep on my rolled-up parka. Even in my sleep, I could hear their words that sounded like coughing and throat clearing. From time to time I heard my name—Al . . . eee—and the sound was comforting.

I woke up suddenly. A boy was squatting in front of me, staring right into my face. He was about my age, and he wore a knitted headband that said "Matu" in red and blue. I sat up, rubbing my eyes. They felt so dry I could hardly blink.

The boy held out his hand near my chin. "Al . . . eee," he said. "You buy *ulu*?"

"*Ulu*?" I said.

"Woman's knife," he said. "*Ulu ipiktuq.*"

He held out a fan-shaped blade. His thick, shiny blue-black hair was swinging against the edge of his jaw. He wore blue jeans and a black jacket like kids at home.

"A knife?" I asked.

"Cut things," he said, motioning with the funny-look-ing knife. "Make clothes. Cut meat. Caribou handle."

The women who had scraped the skins had used the same kind of knife.

"It's nice," I said, not wanting to hurt his feelings. "But I don't need an *ulu*."

"You need *ulu*," he insisted. "I sell cheap."

I shook my head. "No, thank you," I said.

"I make," he said, his lower lip pouting. He stuck the *ulu* into the pocket of his jacket and stood up. He start-ed to walk away.

"Wait," I said. "How do you know so much English?"

He knelt down beside me again. "I go to school on coast last year," he said.

"Then you know about the school? Will you help me find my mother?"

"She lost?" he asked.

"She's a teacher."

"At school?" he asked. "Which school?"

"Well, the school on the coast, I guess," I said.

His blue jeans were tucked inside big, furry boots. The boots smelled sour, but they were fancy, with lacings that were dyed red.

"I was on my way to meet my mother when my plane crashed," I said. "That man over there rescued me."

"My grandfather," he said.

"Will you tell him to take me to my mother?" I asked. "She's waiting for me."

"Coast too far maybe," he said, shrugging his shoulders.

"How can I get there?"

"Dogs. No other way. Snowmobiles all broke."

"Will you *please* ask Ikayauq to take me?" I asked again.

Matu looked over at his sleeping grandfather and shook his head. "Ikayauq must trap," he said. "Ikayauq best trapper in whole village."

He looked down at the floor whenever I looked him in the eyes. He spoke softly like the others, slowly, and without emphasis on any particular word. Everything he said seemed to end in a question, as if he wasn't sure about anything.

"Will you at least ask him?" I said. "I *have* to get home."

"Home?" he asked.

"To my mother," I said. "We really live in California."

"California?" he asked, shivering. "Scary place. I see movie at school. Motorcycles. Kung fu."

"You'd love California," I said. "There's lots of sunshine and beaches."

"We got beaches on coast," he said.

"I didn't know there were beaches in Alaska," I said.

"We got beaches," he said. He studied the dirty floor.

"Why aren't you in school now?" I asked.

"School on coast close last year," he said.

"Well, it's not closed now. My mother's there."

"Teachers steal money. Elders chase them from village with guns."

"Teachers don't steal money," I said.

"Kids save money for a basketball trip to Kotzebue," he said. "Teachers steal money and school close."

"No teacher would ever steal a kid's money," I said.

"Some do, maybe," he said. "*Naluagmi* come and go. Only *Iñupiat* stay."

"What's *Naluagmi*?" I asked.

"White people," he said, wrinkling his nose.

We didn't say anything for a while. I thought I should buy the knife.

"Will *you* take me?" I asked.

"Matu never go so far alone! Al . . . eee only white girl," he said.

"I don't care how far it is," I said. "I've got to get to the coast."

He looked over at his sleeping grandfather while he thought about it.

"Ikayauq take dogs trapping maybe," he said at last.

"There are lots more dogs outside," I said. "Who owns all those dogs?"

He hung his head. "Matu's dogs not as good as Ikayauq's dogs maybe," he said.

"Dogs are dogs," I said. "Do you know the way? Can you get us there?"

He shrugged, fingering the *ulu* in his pocket. He pursed his lips. Then he rocked back and forth on his heels as he squatted in front of me and spoke very slowly. "May . . . be," he said.

6

WHITE-OUT

No one in the village seemed to think it would be any ordeal getting to the coast by dog team, and I expected it to take a day or two. Ikayauq acted more than glad to have the responsibility on someone else's shoulders. My life would be in Matu's hands, and he was only thirteen years old and three inches shorter than me.

I promised I'd build him a better house when I became a famous writer, so that he and Ikayauq wouldn't have to live so poorly.

Matu laughed in my face. "Ikayauq not poor," he said, shaking his head. "Ikayauq rich."

Matu didn't have any idea how poor he was. He was perfectly comfortable in his grandfather's crowded hut. He just threw up his hands and shrugged his shoulders when I tried to tell him about modern conveniences like garbage disposals and dishwashers and garage door openers. He didn't even care about those things.

Mom once pointed out a woman along Pacific Coast Highway. She must have been dressed in everything she owned and she carried a paper sack filled with things she collected as she walked.

"Look, Allison," Mom said. "There's that woman from the Alpha Beta parking lot. Poor thing. I don't understand why our government can't do something. If we can put a man on the moon, surely we can provide for people like that."

A week later she joined a group that raised money to buy condemned houses that were fixed up as shelters. Mom would have been a great missionary. She was always finding projects to work on.

Mom was the one who suggested I help out at the after-school clinic for the deaf. She'd read in the paper how the director needed students to help the kids with their homework.

I told her I was too busy writing in my journal and doing my own homework, but she bought me a book on sign language anyway. Then she talked someone at the clinic into tutoring me in signing.

Mom liked to take charge of my life.

"I have no doubt you'll be a famous writer someday," she said. "But you've got to get out of your shell and walk in another person's shoes if you want to have something to write about."

Eventually, I liked going to the after-school clinic and helping the kids. Mom used to brag to everyone at political fund-raisers how her daughter had learned to sign.

I hadn't written a single word in my journal since I'd crashed in Alaska. There was no privacy in Ikayauq's hut, and I liked to be alone when I wrote personal stuff. I didn't like people peering over my shoulder.

I studied Ikayauq's family while they studied me. The little kids had faces like cherubs, but they needed baths. Their hands and faces were grimy with dirt. I gave them candy bars and bubble gum I'd stuffed in my duffel.

Matu talked with Ikayauq for a long time about the route to the coast. Ikayauq gestured frequently to the sky, as if he expected Matu to navigate by the stars. No one seemed to mind that a thirteen-year-old kid was taking me a long way across the ice. Matu had gone to school on the coast. He knew the way.

Matu's dogs weren't as well trained as Ikayauq's, but Matu's sled was newer, wrapped with fishing line instead of strips of leather. The woman who was Ikayauq's wife made me furry boots like Matu's. "Caribou mukluks," she said. She inverted the piece of skin that was the sole so there was fur against the bottom of my feet. Ikayauq's sister knit me wrist cuffs and a scarf out of colorful wool. She gave me a pair of mittens that were much warmer than my own.

"Beaver," Matu said, admiring them.

The men loaded Matu's sled with frozen fish for the dogs, dried fish and chunks of frozen meat for us, fur skins, canvas tarps, and other supplies for the trail. We took along Matu's gun and my duffel bag and bedroll.

We went a long way the first day, stopping only for short periods of time because the weather was good. I had no idea where we were or in what direction we were going, but I had learned to trust Matu. He drove his team like an expert, even though there were no road signs. He kept his eyes on the horizon. Now and then he looked up at the sky or out at the flat, shiny surfaces that were frozen lakes and ponds. He just *seemed* to know where he was going, and that was good enough for me. It had to be.

We stopped for the night, and Matu knew how to build an igloo as well as his grandfather. It just took him longer.

I helped him stack the icy blocks together, lay the fur skins out on the ground inside, and move the last block of ice in front of the doorway.

He lit the oil lamp, and soon we were cozy.

He chewed on a piece of dried fish, but I wasn't hungry. I crawled into my bedroll with all my clothes on. I was completely exhausted, though I'd ridden on the sled all the way. Even so, I couldn't sleep. I listened to the dogs howling outside and wondered how many wild animals were lurking out there in the distance. I sure wasn't going to let Matu know I was scared. He seemed to think it was a joke that I was from the lower 48. And the fact I was a girl made it an even bigger joke.

He rolled up in fur skins and made himself right at home, as if he didn't have a care in the world.

As soon as he woke up, Matu started getting the dogs ready for the trail. He hit the frisky dogs on their noses and scolded them harshly as he tried to line them up and get them into their harnesses. It seemed to take forever. He kept looking at the sky as if worried about the weather. Twice, the lead dog bolted before we were ready to go. Matu had to chase it down. He waved his arms and shouted, then tackled the dog and started beating it with his fists.

The dog whimpered loudly. "Stop! Stop!" I shouted. "Don't hit that dog!"

Matu kept striking the dog. The poor thing cowered, tail and head down, and dragged itself back into place. Matu got the lines untangled, and the dogs lined up for the third time.

"Too bad Al . . . eee only white girl," he said angrily. "Matu sure need help."

"You don't know how to treat dogs," I said. "Is it always this much work? Maybe you're not doing it right."

"Dogs only pups," he said. "Too young for trail maybe."

"We should have gone by snowmobile," I said.

"Snowmobile no good," he said. "Run out of fuel."

"I saw a snowmobile outside your house," I said. "We could have taken that one, and we could have taken along extra fuel. We'd be to the coast by now."

"That machine my cousin's," he said. "Village council blue-ticket him."

"Blue-ticket? What do you mean?"

"Send out. Elders vote."

"You mean they kicked your cousin out of his own village? What did he do that was so terrible?"

"Rob other man's trap line many times. My cousin lazy man."

At last the dogs started off. They were strong, racing madly across the snow and ice, tails low and shoulders hunching. As the wind increased, the temperature dropped sharply. It had taken Matu too long to get his dogs into position.

My face and hands were already numb. I kept thinking

Matu would get cold and stop, but he didn't. When I finally asked him to stop, he only laughed. There was an envelope of daylight on the horizon. I watched it as we soared across a desert of snow, but the light disappeared after a short time. It was the briefest day I'd ever seen.

"Please stop, Matu," I said.

"*Naluagmi* always cold," he said.

He finally stopped, and we set about building our igloo. We hardly talked when we were inside. It seemed I was always in Matu's way. I was afraid he might turn around and not take me all the way to the coast.

In spite of the beaver mittens, my hands were painfully cold. Feeling came back with a vengeance, and I cried out in pain.

"Ouch! They sting so much!" I said.

Matu was chewing on dried fish. "Good sign maybe," he said.

"Good sign? What do you mean?"

"Pain mean life coming back. Better than freezing."

I put my hands between my knees and rocked back and forth. "It must be terrible to freeze to death," I said.

"Good maybe."

"There can't be anything good about freezing to death," I said. Then I asked, "What does it feel like?"

"Numbness. Sleep. Death. Old people go out on the ice and die sometimes."

"On purpose?"

"Sure."

"You mean, they just freeze to death?"

"Sure. Old person die and bear has good meal. Get fat.

Then son or grandson kill bear. Enough bear to feed whole village maybe. Good idea."

I didn't say anything after that. There was no point trying to talk to someone who thought freezing to death and being eaten by a bear was all right.

Matu was perfectly content, leaning on a fur skin and chewing a chunk of fish. He didn't seem to get cold, and he didn't seem to mind the eerie howling outside, howling that came not only from the dogs and the wind, but also from unseen wolves in the distance.

I couldn't sleep because of the howling. I kept thinking about bears eating frozen old people. I tossed and turned, listening and thinking. I was just dozing off when Matu's voice woke me.

"Al . . . eee! Al . . . eee!"

He was calling from outside. I struggled to the entrance and peered out.

"Al . . . eee! Get gun quick!"

He was standing between his dogs and a monstrous yellow fox that was running toward our camp.

I hesitated, then grabbed Matu's gun.

"Shoot!" Matu shouted.

"I don't know how," I said. "I've never shot a gun in my life."

"Pull hammer," Matu shouted. "Cock! Shoot!"

There hadn't been time to pull on my mittens. My hands were freezing, the fingers stiff, but I closed my eyes and pulled the trigger. There was a deafening explosion. The force knocked me backward, and I fell in the snow.

I missed the fox completely, but the sound made it veer off its course.

Matu ran over and took the gun. He aimed and fired. The fox fell. He hurried over to take a look at it. "Rabid," he shouted.

I was shaking so much I couldn't speak. My ears still rang. I dug my mittens from my parka and pulled them on. The fox lay on the snow, oozing blood.

The dogs yelped and jumped, their icy chains clanking. Matu set fire to the fox to keep the animals from eating it. Then he dug a hole and buried it.

This time, I helped him get the dogs into their harnesses. I had to sneak up from behind and grab one, then straddle its strong, wiggling body, holding with all my strength while Matu fastened the harness. His dogs were younger and didn't seem as vicious as Ikayauq's, but I avoided their snapping jaws.

Matu called his lead dog Amaguq, which he said was Iñupiat for "wolf." Amaguq had watching eyes that glowed in the dark, a salt-and-pepper-colored back, and a snow-colored underside. He held his head high and chased the other dogs to nip at their legs, letting them know he was in charge.

We didn't get very far because of the fierce wind. It whipped at my parka hood and seeped through the crack along my zipper. It lifted snow from the ground and sent it foaming and swirling into the air. I pulled my scarf high across my face. The fur of my ruff helped block the wind and kept the blowing snow out of my eyes. I had to squint to see, but there was nothing to see. Only white above, below, and around us. We were lost in a churning sea of white.

Matu made me get off the sled and walk to keep from

freezing. I didn't argue. He knew how to survive, how to build an igloo, and how to shoot a fox. We struggled through the snow, following the dogs who could hardly walk themselves, staggering against a wall of snowy wind. Fear kept me going.

Matu finally stopped in a place with a rise high enough to block the wind. There was no way we could build an ice house with the wind so strong. I huddled against the wedge of snow while Matu staked and chained the dogs. Then he turned the sled on its side, dumping out all our belongings. He stretched a big canvas tarp over the sled and staked it like a tent, then piled snow on top and around the sides. Within minutes he had a fairly substantial shelter, and we crowded inside. Once the lamp was lit, the furs spread out, and I was deep inside my bedroll, I felt safer. I wanted to go to sleep until the storm passed, but Matu insisted we stay awake.

He left the igloo frequently to walk back and forth outside, and he made me do the same, saying it would keep us from freezing. The dogs curled into balls. Soon they were covered by drifting veils of snow. They didn't bark. They didn't howl. The only sound we could hear was the savage wind.

Once the wind swept snow over the shelter and buried it completely, it was as snug and airtight as any igloo. The lamp sent out rays of warmth. Matu didn't think we should risk going to sleep, so he leaned back on his elbows and told me about Maniilaq, a nineteenth-century Iñupiat who predicted that the white man would come and bring many changes.

"Maniilaq say men fly in sky on iron sled and travel in boat without paddle," he said. "He say people wear new kind of clothes and write on thin birch bark and talk through air."

"How could someone know all that?" I asked.

"Maniilaq magic maybe," Matu said. "Maniilaq Iñupiat prophet."

"Well, you can believe what you want," I said. "It sounds phony to me."

I chewed on a piece of dried fish as Matu talked. It was as stiff as cardboard at first. As it softened, it had a greasy, rotten flavor. Matu's voice droned on like a lazy afternoon, and I almost forgot the freezing dogs and the howling wind.

Matu told how Maniilaq broke taboos set by the shaman. It was hard to believe, but people in the old days actually thought if they cut and tanned a caribou hide during fishing season, they would die.

"Maniilaq break shaman's rules," Matu said. "He never die. He live."

Matu said that Maniilaq showed people how mixing foods from the sea and foods from the land wouldn't kill them, even though the shaman had warned them otherwise.

"Restaurants serve surf and turf all the time," I said.

"Shaman boss people in old days," Matu said.

Then Matu told me something unbelievable. The ancient Iñupiats put pregnant women in snow huts to deliver their own babies! He said Maniilaq changed all that.

Matu *still* lived in the Dark Ages as far as I was concerned. He'd never even eaten a pizza or ridden a surfboard or gone to Disneyland. He had a blank look on his face when I told him about some of my favorite rock groups.

"California terrible place," he said.

He started to shake as if just thinking about California gave him the creeps.

"California's the best place in the United States," I said.

"I see California movie at school," he said. "Lots of killing."

"That's only the movies. People don't go around doing that in Dana Point."

"Dana Point?"

"That's where I live. Haven't you ever heard of Richard Henry Dana? Everybody has to read *Two Years Before the Mast* in English. You must have heard of him."

He just watched my mouth move as if I were speaking some foreign language.

"Well, at least you don't have to take algebra or put up with freeway traffic just to go to the mall," I said.

I pulled my old teddy bear out of my duffel to use as a pillow, and Matu went crazy laughing. He'd never heard of Winnie the Pooh. It made me wonder about his childhood. I mean, didn't he even have toys or stuffed animals?

We waited for the weather to improve. We slept, ate the disgusting fish, and talked a little. Then we slept again. There was no way to know if it was day or night. Matu said we'd been there three days, but that could have been a wild guess. We took turns going outside to walk back and forth, go to the bathroom, and check on the dogs. They were buried in snow. They lay curled, their noses tucked under their tails, as still as death.

7

CHILD OF THE ICE WORM

When things got really boring, I wrote in my journal. I wrote a letter to Mom, figuring I'd copy it later and mail it.

"Dear Mom,

I'll never, *ever* forgive you. I just looked in my mirror, and sure enough, there's a pimple on my forehead! A pimple! Me! Remember how you used to tell me I had a perfect peaches-and-cream complexion? Not anymore, thanks to you!

I know why I have the pimple. It's because my hair is filthy dirty and hanging down into my face. You *know* how I have to shampoo and condition my hair every single day! How could you do this to me? I'm your daughter!

My lips are so chapped they're cracked and blistered. It's raw under my nose from just breathing! The steam from my breath freezes on my face, and when it melts or I rub it away with my smelly, filthy mitten, my face gets redder and more chapped.

I'm risking my life wandering through snow blizzards

because someone in this crazy, mixed-up family has got to do something to save the Atwoods, not that you care anymore.

Your daughter, Allison"

When I finished Mom's letter, I was warmed up enough to write a letter to Dad. I had to be careful how I worded things to Dad. He had a habit of misinterpreting everything I said. Sometimes an innocent remark would lead to an hour of cross-examination. It took a lot to impress him or get his attention. His mind was always somewhere else.

"Dear Dad,

I'm dashing off a note to say this is a wonderful experience. I feel like I'm in the middle of a *National Geographic* special on TV. I only wish I'd brought along your movie camera. You've probably heard by now about the plane crash and my rescue. Even though the pilot was killed instantly and I nearly froze to death, I don't want you to worry. I'm currently risking my life traveling across Alaska with a thirteen-year-old Eskimo boy via dog team, taking notes on the native people and their culture.

Your daughter, Allison of the Arctic"

I closed my journal and tucked it away inside my duffel so no one could read it. Matu was getting on my nerves. He didn't seem uncomfortable about not brushing his teeth or washing his face. I was bored to tears and restless, but not Matu. He just let the weather determine his life. He could kick back and relax as if he were on a picnic. It didn't matter to him that we were cooped up in a stuffy, cramped snow shelter day after day when there were miles left to go.

I pulled my tape player from my duffel and listened to some of my music. Matu wrinkled his nose. Then I got out one of my shirts that had a picture of my favorite group. Their faces were on the front, their rear ends on the back, and it was decorated with a lot of sequins. Matu wasn't impressed. He fiddled with the sequins until some came off in his hand, but he didn't ask any questions about the group or the music they played.

I tried to tell him how some of the groups got together and how much money they made on concert tours, but he wasn't interested.

I even tried to explain a dance I'd made up that went with one of my favorite songs. Facing backward, roll right shoulder four times, left shoulder four times. Stomp and whirl. Clap!

The dance went on for three full minutes, the entire length of the song, but I stopped describing it after about thirty seconds because Matu was laughing. It was no use. You can't describe a dance. You have to *demonstrate* it, and there was no room in the cramped shelter to do that.

"We dance at school last year," Matu said. "Teachers bring music."

"Don't Eskimos dance?" I asked.

"Sure, we dance. Drums only."

"Like Indians?" I asked.

He made a face and turned away. The batteries in my tape player got weak. The music dragged, the voices sounding warped and funny, then stopping altogether.

"What's wrong with Indians?" I asked.

He didn't answer. He just sulked.

I pulled my journal out once again and wrote about Matu, about how poor he was and how he didn't know anything about the real world, not even the American Indians. If he'd studied any history, he'd know how white settlers had taken over their land and mistreated them, and he wouldn't have such a negative view. What he needed was more exposure to the outside world. He'd never even seen a mall or gone to a concert or owned a surfboard. He'd never even heard of the Rolling Stones or Patty Hearst or Jimmy Carter.

Time dragged. We went outside and walked around in a big circle. We threw fish to the dogs. Then we crawled back into that miserable little mound of snow and ice that had become our home. It was like being buried alive.

Finally, the wind stopped. Matu rallied the dogs, and we hurriedly repacked the sled. Even though we worked fast, it took a long time.

Daylight was the color of mother-of-pearl. It came in the middle of the day, peeking through as if a window shade had been slightly raised. As we traveled, the landscape changed. Then, it seemed we crossed an invisible line. Before there hadn't even been a weed, and now suddenly there were trees on the slopes and in the ravines.

After a while, Matu guided the dogs to a frozen river. We continued for hours upon the flat ice. Then, in the distance, I saw children playing in the snow. They were sliding down a bank on sheets of metal. A dog team passed by going in the opposite direction, and the man on the back runner waved. Near the village, a fat gray-haired woman pulled fish from a hole cut in the ice. The fish twisted and jerked on the line, then froze in mid-air, fins stretched out like wings. With her bare hands, the woman yanked one fish after another off the fishing line. She didn't even wince from the cold.

A boy carried two pails of water he'd taken from a hole in the ice. The buckets hung from a yoke across his shoulders. Water sloshed over the rims of the buckets and froze on the snow as he struggled up the slope.

Men on snowmobiles roared past and raced across the frozen river. Boys carrying rifles and dead white birds walked along the banks. As Matu's team climbed the riverbank toward the cluster of houses, village dogs snarled and paced upon yellow ice.

"Where are we?" I asked.

Matu didn't answer.

Laundry hung on lines, trouser legs and shirt arms kicking and waving stiffly in the wind. Smoke rose from little pipes that jutted from the rooftops of about thirty huts. Outside every hut there was a snowmobile, piles of antlers, blue oil drums, abandoned stove parts, and all kinds of useless junk.

"Is this the coast?" I asked.

"Halfway maybe," Matu said.

"Only halfway! I can't believe we've only come halfway!"

It was a much bigger village than Ikayauq's. I was ready for a decent bed to sleep in, a hot shower, and a large combination pizza.

"Can we stop here and rest awhile?" I asked.

"Sure," he said.

Matu took us to his cousin's hut, and Sikik gave us caribou soup.

Sikik didn't like me very much. I could tell by the way she kept glancing sideways at me. I tried smiling at her and being as polite as I could, but it didn't help. She spoke Iñupiat to Matu, and I heard my name mentioned over and over.

"Why doesn't she like me?" I asked.

"Al . . . eee only white girl," he said.

"I can't help that," I said.

He concentrated on his soup.

I slept on the floor between two giggly children who tried to pinch freckles off my skin and brush the sun streaks from my hair. Paniyapluk, especially, never left my side. Even when I washed my face with hot water from the stove, she stood close by to watch me.

"Spots not come off," she said, giggling and pointing.

"She speaks English," I said to Matu.

"Paniyapluk learn from brothers," he said.

Paniyapluk was about five or six, the older of Sikik's two smallest girls, and she had a perfectly round face and the shiniest black hair I'd ever seen.

Paniyapluk and her little sisters were so grimy with dirt I felt guilty about using their water. Sikik was pregnant and had other children, one around Matu's age and a few even older. It was hard to tell how many children she had because kids kept coming and going in and out of the hut, and everyone acted as if they belonged there.

Sikik didn't have running water or electricity, but she had more things than Ikayauq. Her hut was bigger, and she had some furniture. There was a table and four chairs, and beds were pushed against the wall so that people could sit on them when no one was sleeping.

She had a calendar tacked up on the wall, a dirty throw rug on the floor, and a shelf that sloped beneath the weight of mail order catalogs. Paniyapluk got the catalogs down from the shelf to show me that Sikik could buy just about anything she wanted through the mail. The pages were frayed from so many turnings.

Sikik looked away when I smiled at her, but Paniyapluk's father, Aqsuk, *really* didn't like me. He came into the hut, tobacco bulging inside his cheek, and he sat with his back to me chewing the ugly brown stuff.

Aqsuk had high cheekbones that caught the light, an extremely flat nose, and very slanted eyes. At least four of his front teeth were missing, and the ones remaining were stained brown. The ice around Sikik's front door was black from his spit. He drank soda all day long and threw empty cans onto a pile outside the hut.

I don't know if he was the father of all of Sikik's children, but he was definitely Paniyapluk's father, and he came to sleep in Sikik's hut whenever he wanted. One of his jobs was to climb the rickety ladder to the food cache. It was a shack that looked like a doghouse set up high on tall stakes. Matu said Sikik kept her meat there away from wild animals, especially wolverines. Aqsuk went up into the food cache and carried down big chunks of caribou, moose, or bear for Sikik to cook.

Matu didn't seem in any hurry to repack the sled or get his dogs ready to go. He lounged around outside, sitting on an empty oil drum as if he had forever to get to the coast. When I asked him why we weren't leaving, he said he wasn't going any farther.

"But you promised!" I said. "I can't stay here."

"Lots of ptarmigan now," he said.

"What's ptarmigan?"

He laughed and slapped a knee. "Al . . . eee not know ptarmigan!" he said. "Ptarmigan bird! Ptarmigan food!"

"You promised to take me to the coast," I said. "Look, I'll pay you. I've got money. I'll pay whatever you ask."

"Matu not for sale. Dogs not for sale either."

He looked down at the dirty ice near his feet. Some of the boys smirked. They looked tough, but when I looked directly at them, they turned away grinning shyly.

"Al . . . eee catch mail plane maybe," he said.

The boys laughed and spat tobacco juice on the snow.

"When does the plane come?" I asked.

"Tomorrow maybe."

"Tomorrow?"

"When weather good," he said.

"It's good now," I said. "I mean, it's good enough."

"Mail plane come last week," a boy said.

"How about tomorrow? Will it come tomorrow?"

"Maybe."

Sikik came outside. She was bundled in a parka-dress that was decorated with red rickrack. "Iñupiat on coast not like white girl maybe," she said. She pursed her lips and looked toward the sky. "*Naluagmi* bad for Iñupiat!"

59

She tied a flowered bandanna around her head. It didn't match anything she was wearing. She didn't put on makeup, and she just let her hair hang into her eyes.

Paniyapluk tugged on my parka sleeve, and her little sisters stood at her side.

"White peoples come from ice worm," she said.

I shivered and looked down at her. "Ice worm! What's that?"

"Worm in glacier," she said. Her eyes twinkled. "Ice worm all white." She wrinkled her nose.

The boys whispered behind their hands. Some of Sikik's neighbors came out of their huts and clustered in groups, chattering in low, harsh tones and glancing sideways at me.

One girl, however, stood off by herself. I noticed her on a knoll, bent and crooked like a tree twisted by the wind. From where I stood, I couldn't see what she looked like, but I knew something was not right about her. When she saw me looking her way, she moved out of sight, one of her legs dragging behind her.

"Who's that?" I asked, and I motioned to the spot where she had been.

Everyone heard me. I'd spoken loud enough. Sikik pulled up her parka hood with a grumble. The boys looked in the other direction. Matu examined the toe of his mukluk.

Then Paniyapluk answered. "That only Oolik," she said.

"Who's Oolik?" I asked.

Again, no one answered. Matu went over to check his

restless dogs. Sikik walked to a neighbor's house. The boys got ready to go hunting. No one explained about Oolik, not even Paniyapluk.

Paniyapluk pulled me back inside the hut because she was anxious to go through my duffel. She scribbled on some pages of my journal and sorted through my lipsticks and nail polish as if they were pieces of candy. She laughed when she saw my teddy bear, and she shook my shampoo until it was full of bubbles. She demanded that I put my dangly earrings on her ears as she slid about a dozen bracelets on her small arm.

"You present me?" she asked.

She held up her arm to admire the jewelry, and she looked in the mirror to study the earrings. I didn't know what to give her, so I gave her a little pink soap that was shaped like a rose. She held it to her nose and sniffed it suspiciously. Then she stuck her tongue against the soap and made a face.

"It's soap," I said. "You can wash your face and hands with it and smell pretty."

She put it into her pocket without saying thank you, then found my cassettes. I explained that the batteries in my tape player were dead. She got the batteries out of Sikik's flashlight.

"Matu say you dance," she said, pulling on my hands. "Al . . . eee, come! Teach dance."

I promised I'd teach her to dance if she'd show me where to buy a plane ticket to the coast. She hurried into her furry parka with the beaver mittens attached at the cuffs. She led the way through the village to a wooden building painted dark green. It was the store, no bigger than Dad's bedroom. In the center stood a big black oil stove. Shelves were loaded with dusty cans of soup and sauces, sacks of rice, boxes of Pilot Boy bread, Coke, Pepsi, candy, dry cereal, gum, and cartons of cigarettes. There were no fruits or vegetables, no meat or dairy products, no refrigerated or frozen foods. Wool shirts, rubber boots, ropes, and aluminum buckets hung from the ceiling. On the wall behind the counter were guns and ammunition.

A man about Dad's age was sitting on a stool. Under his padded vest he wore a plaid shirt. The cuffs were rolled up, showing the sleeves of his longjohns. His eyes were hidden behind tinted, gold-rimmed glasses. He said something in Iñupiat to Paniyapluk and, as usual, she giggled.

"I need to get to the coast," I said. "I'd like to buy a plane ticket."

"Is Matu giving up on his dogs already?" the man asked. His English was perfect.

"He wants to go hunting for ptarmigan," I said.

"Too bad," the man said. "That takes priority, I suppose, to getting a white girl to the coast. It's a long trip, probably too long for a boy like Matu."

"I've got to get there," I said. "How safe is the plane? Is it real small?"

He laughed. "You must be Allison," he said. "My name's Igri. That means John in English. Welcome to my village."

"You know me?"

"Ah, yes. Matu told me about you," he said.

"When *exactly* does the mail plane come?" I asked.

"Never exactly," he said.

"What do you mean?"

"It depends on the weather."

"How will I know when it comes?" I asked.

"When you hear it buzz the village," he said. "A plane always buzzes the village before it lands. Unless it's a liquor plane. A liquor plane doesn't buzz the village."

"Why not?"

"This is a dry village. Planes fly in liquor after we receive our government checks."

"Sikik get drunk sometimes," Paniyapluk said. "Aqsuk always. Matu's mother go under house and die."

Paniyapluk gazed up at me with those almond-shaped eyes and didn't crack a smile.

"Matu's mother died?"

"She froze to death," John said. "Matu was two years old. His grandparents adopted him. Paniyapluk heard about it in the family. We have no secrets here."

"That's awful!"

"She was seventeen. She got drunk once too often," he said. "Life's not easy here. The times have taken a toll on our spirit."

John talked about how his family had migrated with the seasons to hunt, trap, and fish, living in tents in the summer and sod houses in the winter. He told how he'd struggled through schools set up by the Bureau of Indian Affairs and the missionaries. He said that he eventually left the village and attended the University of Alaska.

63

"Education's important, but not at the expense of anyone's identity as an Iñupiat," he said.

All the time he was talking, I was thinking of how Matu's mother had frozen to death under the house.

"But what about Matu's mother?" I asked.

"She was confused," he said. "Her life had no meaning. I guess a white girl from the lower forty-eight wouldn't understand."

Paniyapluk tugged on my parka.

"I have to get out of here," I said. "Do you take traveler's checks?"

"When you hear the plane circle low over the rooftops, you'll have plenty of time to come get your ticket and walk to the landing strip."

"Where's that?"

He pointed. "Right out there on the river," he said. It looked like a silver ribbon in the moonlight. "We'll have to unload the plane before you can board. Don't worry about your ticket until then."

"Do you have a phone? My mom will be worried."

"No phones. I have a radio, but it's dead at the moment. Sorry."

On the way back to Sikik's hut, we passed the cemetery. The earth seemed bald; the snow swept away by gusts of wind. The full moon was huge and it made the sky glow pink. The grave markers shimmered eerily in the moonlight. Weathered white, the narrow obelisks were made out of wooden two-by-four stakes.

I heard a strange sound and whirled around quickly. A figure stood at a distance. Someone had been following us.

"Oolik," Paniyapluk said.

As we walked past the cemetery, I could hear the scrape of Oolik's leg.

I turned again, trying to catch sight of her. Oolik stopped, keeping far enough away so that I couldn't see her face.

"Al . . . eee, go!" Paniyapluk said impatiently. "It only Oolik. She's being funny."

The cemetery was the highest point of the village. Below were the huts, almost invisible amongst the thin strip of trees, and below them, the river.

"Is Matu's mother buried here?" I asked.

"Lots of peoples," she said.

Names were carved on the wooden markers. Many of the markers had early death dates.

"Was there an epidemic or something?" I asked.

"Huh?"

"Was there a disease, you know, a sickness that killed a lot of people?"

"Bad sickness maybe," she said. "Girls take off clothes and die in snow. One brother hanged himself."

"I'm sorry," I said.

"Jonas lazy," she said. "Not hunt even. One day he quit."

"How old was he?"

"Sixteen maybe," she said. "Aqsuk cut him down."

Nothing seemed real in the eerie light of day that was more like night. Not the graves. Not Paniyapluk. Not even me.

I stared at the wooden stakes, a sad sight beneath that monstrous moon.

8

OOLIK

When Sikik left the house, I wrote in my journal. I didn't write about the Eskimos. I wrote about my parents. Writing helped me figure things out.

Mom once marched for civil rights, but that wasn't the mom I knew. My mom had bleached blonde hair that she curled and piled high. She wore false eyelashes and had her nails wrapped and bought jewelry that was real gold. Her hobby, in fact, was shopping. She went to the mall at least three times a week because Dad worked late. Even though she went to Lawyers' Wives' meetings, did volunteer work in the community, and hired caterers for parties, she usually managed to pick me up on time or a few minutes early.

Dad was Dad. Political, preoccupied, and predictable. He was always late or he forgot entirely. His idea of a great present was to toss his credit card on the table and say, "Buy yourself something." He argued about the slightest thing, and when Mom or I got upset he'd say, "I'm only playing the devil's advocate." Dad's favorite topic of conversation was his latest big win in court. He referred to Mom and me as "you women." "You women don't appreciate how hard I work just so you can shop and throw money away." He lumped us together with his secretaries and the cleaning lady and the court reporters and waitresses and file clerks and, well, just women in general. You women!

When I was twelve, Mom joined a consciousness-raising group and started talking about women's rights, her rights in particular. That was when Dad became a male chauvinist, according to Mom, and, according to Dad, that was the beginning of the end. It was the consciousness-raising group that put those crazy ideas into Mom's head about finding herself. Mom started taking an interest in the environment. She stopped going with Dad to fund-raisers for candidates she didn't like. She said if she were young and single she'd join the Peace Corps, and that's when she signed me up to help at the after-school clinic.

Sikik came back inside, and I put away my journal.

"Mail plane not come," she said.

"The weather looks good enough," I said.

"Storm somewhere, maybe," she said.

"How do you know?"

She didn't answer, so I put on my parka and went down to the store to check with John.

"The weather's unpredictable, especially this time of year," he said.

"My mother will be worried," I said.

"Teachers don't last long in the Arctic," he said.

"Because of the weather?"

"Maybe," he said.

"Because they miss home?"

"Perhaps," he said.

"My mom's a good teacher. She teaches kids origami."

"Origami? What's that?"

"Paper folding," I said.

He chuckled and lit a cigarette. His tinted glasses reflected the flame of the wooden match. "Now, that's real important, I suppose. That's just what we need. Paper folding."

Aqsuk came into his store with some men. Two women entered behind him. John spoke to them in Iñupiat. Sometimes he used Iñupiat and English in the same sentence. He gave people credit. They bought things and didn't pay for them. He just wrote down their names. Everyone was asking about the mail plane, but John said he didn't think the mail plane was coming.

Matu and the boys returned with enough ptarmigan for the entire village.

Sikik sat on the floor of the hut to pluck out feathers. She cut off the heads and the big, furry feet.

I wasn't expecting to eat any part of a bird with furry feet, but it smelled good when Sikik cooked it. It tasted like the rock cornish game hens Mom fixed one Christmas. Soon I was eating a ptarmigan leg and licking the grease off my fingers like everyone else.

The tasty meal put Matu in a good mood, so I asked him to take me the rest of the way to the coast.

"Bad weather maybe," he said. "Not good for dogs."

"You just don't want to go," I said.

"Mail plane come tomorrow maybe," he said.

The next morning I repacked my duffel, but the mail plane didn't come.

Aqsuk laughed and spat tobacco juice on the ice just inches from my feet before wandering off.

"Maybe tomorrow," John said.

"And maybe not," I said.

That night I dreamt about Dad's condo. It was enormous. The sand-colored plush pile carpeting stretched out forever, like an endless beach. He had a stained-glass window above the front door with sailboats drifting on a kaleidoscope sea. The window was beautiful but served no purpose.

When I awoke, I tried to figure out what was practical and beautiful at the same time. Matu's mukluks, for example, were huge and furry and kept his feet warm even in the coldest weather, even in white-outs. They smelled sour, of course, but they were far nicer than Sikik's or Paniyapluk's or John's, and much better than the pair Ikayauq's wife had made for me. The stitching was exact, the trim bright, the fur long and rich. It surprised me that I'd once thought them ugly.

Paniyapluk wanted to know what was rolled up inside the long shipping tube. I took it out of her hands and put it under my bed roll. There was no point in explaining. She'd never heard of my favorite rock groups.

When Paniyapluk put on my white boots with silver spurs, they looked flimsy compared to Matu's mukluks. They'd cost Dad a fortune, too, even though he didn't know it yet. In fact, he probably hadn't even gotten the credit card bill. I let her walk around in them until Matu came back. Then I made her take them off, and stuffed them inside my duffel.

During the day, Sikik visited neighbors, and Matu left to track caribou. Aqsuk, as usual, was gone. Only Paniyapluk stayed with me.

"You dance me," she said.

"Dance?"

"Matu say you know dance," she said. "You dance me."

"Oh, all right. Get the batteries," I said. She hurried to get the batteries out of Sikik's flashlight.

Facing backward, I rolled my right shoulder four times. One, two, three, four. I rolled the left shoulder. One, two, three, four. Then I whirled around and clapped. I hustled back, snapping my fingers. . . .

Suddenly, there was the bang of the outside door. I froze, thinking Sikik or Aqsuk had returned. Then I heard the scrape of Oolik's leg. The inner door opened.

My breath caught. "Oh! You startled me!"

Paniyapluk pulled on the sleeve of my sweater to get me to continue, but all I could do was stare at Oolik.

From one side, she looked perfectly normal. From the other, she didn't. Looking at her head-on, face-to-face, was like looking at two people at once. Her face was distorted, as if one side had melted. I tried to focus on the normal brown eye and smooth cheek, but my eyes kept returning to the other side of her face, to the watery eye and sagging cheek.

Her useless leg stuck out behind and seemed to prop her up. She wore a filthy parka, and her stringy hair hung into the collar.

My throat was so dry it was difficult to swallow. I knew she was lame. I didn't know she was so horribly ugly.

"Hello," I said, my voice small and shaky. I tried to smile. Oolik looked at me with that pathetic eye, and said nothing.

"Oolik all funny," Paniyapluk said.

I wanted her to go away. I didn't want her to come inside the hut. Then I flooded with shame. "Maybe she wants to dance with us," I said.

Oolik stood rooted to the spot, looking at me sideways and waiting for me to make the first move.

"Not Oolik," Paniyapluk said.

Oolik moaned, head to one side, chin jutting forward. Her fist was doubled up as if she wanted to slug me. She tried to talk. Strange sounds came out.

"Is Oolik deaf?" I asked.

"Oolik funny," Paniyapluk said. "Funny face. Funny leg. Funny ears." She held up her hands to stop Oolik from coming closer. Then she scolded her the way Matu scolded his dogs. "Oolik! Go home! Oolik go!"

Oolik's face contorted all the more. I thought she might cry.

"Don't be mean," I said to Paniyapluk. "Let her stay."

"No! Oolik not visit!"

I held out a hand to let Oolik know it was all right to come inside Sikik's hut. She looked around cautiously, her lower jaw moving as she ground her teeth together.

The tape ended and the player clicked off. Paniyapluk was furious. "No dance!"

I knelt down and rewound the tape. Then I motioned

for Oolik to come and dance. I pressed the button, and the music started again.

Facing backward, I rolled my right shoulder four times, then the left shoulder four times. Paniyapluk pouted, but she copied what I did. She didn't like Oolik watching. I whirled around and clapped. Then I hustled backward with a snap, snap, snap. I slid to the right—one, two, three—and slid to the left—one, two, three.

Paniyapluk was like a shadow, following my every move. Oolik watched, a crooked smile on her face.

After we'd finished, I turned the volume up as high as it would go. Oolik looked down at her good foot, and her face sort of lit up. She could feel the vibration beneath her feet. The music was too loud, but it had to be for Oolik to feel the beat.

Paniyapluk put her hands over her ears and made a face.

"Come on, Oolik," I said, motioning with my hands. "Roll your right shoulder four times. One, two, three, four. Roll your left shoulder four times. One, two, three, four. Now whirl around and clap."

Paniyapluk started dancing to show off for Oolik.

Over and over, I played the tape. Soon Oolik was actually trying to dance.

I lined them up, one on either side of me, and we tried it again and again. Paniyapluk went too fast for the beat, and Oolik was too slow as she dragged her useless leg, stomped her good foot, and clapped her hands. After a while, all three of us were laughing and enjoying ourselves.

Then Sikik came in.

She ignored Paniyapluk and me and went over and

stood directly in front of Oolik, scolding her harshly in Iñupiat. I stopped the tape and took out the batteries.

Oolik made angry gestures with her fist. Then, grimacing, she slowly disappeared through the doors of the hut.

"It's my fault," I said, handing the batteries to Sikik. "I invited Oolik inside. I was teaching Paniyapluk to dance."

"Not Oolik!" Sikik said.

"I feel sorry for her," I said. "No one likes her."

"Oolik steal candy from Paniyapluk and other girls. Oolik bad."

"She's deaf," I said.

"Oolik only crippled girl," Sikik said. "No good." She made a motion with her hands as if to throw Oolik away. Then Sikik sent us out of the house so she could have some peace and quiet.

Paniyapluk and I walked to the store. By the time we got there, John already knew about the dance lesson.

"Not much hope for Oolik," he said. "They put her on the ice when she was born, but the preacher made them take her back."

"She'd have frozen to death on the ice," I said.

"That was the point," John said. "Well, the preacher's long gone, and Oolik's ten, maybe even eleven by now, and no use to her family. She can't fetch water or haul in fish. She's a stubborn girl. She even refuses to make bark baskets."

"But she's crippled and deaf," I said.

"She's lucky to be alive," he said. "In the old days, the crippled were put out on the ice to die. Some old people still try to go out on the ice when their time comes."

"What's going to happen to Oolik?"

"I wish I knew."

I left the store without saying good-bye. No one seemed to care about Oolik. Paniyapluk had to run to catch up with me. I walked uphill to the cemetery and then went farther to a small building that was boarded up.

"That old school," Paniyapluk said.

"Why isn't it open?"

"Teachers always go," she said.

I tromped around the building, and Paniyapluk followed me like a faithful puppy.

"Oolik's okay," I said. "Don't be mean to her."

Paniyapluk folded her arms, pouting. "You dance me?" she asked.

"Will you be nice to Oolik?" I asked.

"You dance Oolik?"

"Maybe," I said. "We'll see."

She wouldn't budge when I started to walk back to Sikik's.

"Come on," I said.

"No!" she said.

I went a few steps farther. Paniyapluk was just a little kid, but she was my only friend. I didn't want to leave her behind.

"Please," I said. "Don't be stubborn."

"Oolik dance . . . maybe," she said, giving in.

I took her hand and we walked together.

When Sikik and her family visited neighbors, Oolik appeared. She waited inside the little enclosed porch they called a cunnychuck. We were like spies from different countries meeting to exchange messages. I decided to teach Oolik my secret language, the language of the hands, the language I'd learned at Mom's insistence when I'd worked at the clinic for the deaf.

9

SIGNING

Sikik's sons provided for her because Aqsuk was a lazy man. They hunted caribou and set trap lines. Aqsuk leaned against an empty oil drum outside, looking angry.

Aqsuk had been expecting an order from Anchorage. He grumbled when Sikik tore a page off her calendar. *Khil ghich Tut Kat.* March. *The summer hawk has come.* I'd left Dad before Valentine's Day, and now it was the middle of March. The days were still short enough to doze through, and the nights were as long as three or four put together. It was hard to keep track of time. Everyone waited for the mail plane to come. Everyone in the village, even the kids, got a regular government check they could spend any way they liked. Aqsuk liked to order things through the mail. The only thing he liked better was to ride around on his snowmobile.

Paniyapluk was Aqsuk's favorite. He tried to wrestle with her, but he played too rough.

Paniyapluk always ran away, hiding behind me or Sikik. Sometimes Sikik scolded Aqsuk and put an end to the roughhousing. Then Aqsuk would sulk in a corner for hours.

It was difficult to tell just how many children Sikik had. At least three were staying in another village with relatives. After I counted seven, another child belonging to Sikik showed up. They didn't all live at home. They stayed with different families in the village.

I tried to help with the chores so Sikik wouldn't mind having me around. I carried water up the slope from the river and cut meat for the soup pot and watched after the youngest kids.

Matu's dogs sat on their chains until he threw them fish. He didn't bother to harness them and take them for a run. John criticized Matu for not exercising the dogs and keeping them properly trained.

Every time I went to the store, John was fiddling with his radio.

"It's only got a range of twenty-five miles," he said. "But on a good day I can reach a neighboring village."

"Can you fix it?" I asked.

"I'm trying," he said. "Atmospheric conditions cause interference, and we've had some spectacular sky shows lately."

"You mean those green lights?" I asked.

He nodded. "The aurora borealis can affect an old model like mine."

"This is an emergency," I said.

"The tundra telegraph is the best we can do," he said.

"What's that?" I asked.

He pointed to the radio. "You're looking at it," he said.

Days passed and John's radio was still dead. I could hardly remember what my house looked like in Dana Point. I tried to describe it to Paniyapluk, but the rooms seemed to blur as I thought about them. I told Paniyapluk about my horse collection and the wallpaper with horses on it. She wrinkled her nose. She'd never seen a horse.

I remembered how dust collected on those horses. Now my life before Dana Point seemed dusty and far away, like a dream.

Oolik followed us wherever we went. Sometimes Paniyapluk's little sisters, bundled into furry balls, tagged along. We walked around the village beneath an enormous moon. The girls were like shadows. When I fell asleep, I sometimes dreamt of them. And I wrote about them in my journal.

When I couldn't stand it, I heated some water on Sikik's stove and shampooed my hair in a bucket.

"Hair might freeze!" Paniyapluk said.

I dried my hair with my Dana Point beach towel, since I couldn't plug in my hair dryer. Oolik drank some of my shampoo, then spat it out. Bubbles foamed around her mouth.

I told Paniyapluk to wash her hands, always sticky from the jawbreakers she bought at John's store. I tried to tell Oolik to wash, too, but she didn't understand.

"Water," I said, pointing to the brown river water in the pail.

Oolik wrinkled her nose and grunted.

I poured some water over Oolik's hands. She wiped them on her parka.

I dipped a cup into Sikik's barrel and scooped out some

water, then I poured the contents of the cup back into the barrel. I raised three fingers and made the hand sign for "water," and motioned for Oolik to imitate me.

Oolik lifted a hand and made the sign. Her face brightened. I clapped my hands to let her know she'd done well. I got out the washing pan and poured some water into it.

"What Al . . . eee do?" Paniyapluk asked.

"I'm showing Oolik how to talk," I said.

"Oolik no talk," Paniyapluk said.

"She can talk with her hands," I said.

"What Oolik say?"

"Water."

"Water?"

I scrubbed my hands with soap, then moved my hands up and down in front of my face. I made the sign for "wash." Oolik watched, then cautiously made the sign. Day after day we sat on the floor of Sikik's hut, and I taught Oolik more words.

I held the fingers of my right hand to my lips, then a flat palm against my right cheek—"eat" and "sleep"— meaning "home." We practiced for hours. I taught her signs for "cook" and "soup." I put my thumb up as if to grab an imaginary brim of a cap, meaning "boy." I taught her phrases like "how are you?" and "he saw me" and "be careful," and then I showed her how to sign numbers.

I drew pictures and wrote words beside them. I held my hands up, swayed them back and forth, and puffed up my cheeks, blowing. Paniyapluk laughed, but Oolik pointed toward the door and puffed up her lopsided cheeks. She'd learned the sign for "storm."

Then Matu came in, and Oolik put her hands in her lap and looked down. "Why Oolik here?" Matu asked. Snow dropped from his boots onto the floor.

"She only visit," Paniyapluk said. "Oolik stay."

Matu helped himself to some caribou soup. He sat on the floor, the bowl in his hands, and watched Oolik. He'd changed since we'd come to the village. He chewed tobacco or raced snowmobiles. He hardly paid any attention to Amaguq or his other dogs. Amaguq nipped the dogs' heels or bit them on the ears. Matu didn't even care.

"Sikik say you put ideas in Oolik's head," he said.

"What kind of ideas?" I asked.

He shrugged. "You not a teacher."

"I can teach her to sign."

"Why sign?"

"So she can talk," I said. "So people can talk to her."

Matu laughed and dipped the spoon into his soup.

Oolik wouldn't raise her eyes from her clasped hands.

Matu sat comfortably on the floor, his smelly mukluks stretched out in front of him, as if he had all day. "Go ahead," he said. "Teach."

"Not with you sitting there," I said. "She doesn't want anyone watching."

"Paniyapluk watch. Paniyapluk think she *Naluagmi* maybe?"

"Oolik's used to Paniyapluk. She's embarrassed because you're watching."

"Oolik never go to school on coast," he said.

"She's learning fast," I said.

"Go on," he said. "Teach."

Oolik wouldn't look up. I tugged at her locked hands, and she shook her head. I pointed to Matu and made the sign for "boy," then spelled out b-o-y. Oolik looked at Matu. He was grinning and slurping his soup noisily.

"Oolik never learn."

I pulled on Oolik's hands. She inhaled, then raised a hand. She made some signs, copying what I'd shown her, but repeating it again with something more. It made me laugh.

"What she say?" Paniyapluk asked.

"She talk about me?" Matu asked.

"She says you're a stupid boy," I said.

"Stupid? Why stupid?"

Matu set his bowl down on the floor and crawled close to squint at Oolik's face. "How she say that?" he asked. "With hands?"

"Yes. I told you she can talk with her hands."

"Why she say Matu stupid?" he asked.

"I don't know."

"Ask her."

"No."

"Why not?"

"I don't want to."

Matu stood up. "Oolik not learn." He stomped out of the hut, banging the doors behind him.

Sikik came in after that with some of her children and the women who were her neighbors. They chattered in

Iñupiat as Sikik rubbed her pregnant belly. She was doing that a lot lately, as if she hurt from carrying around the extra weight. Oolik slipped away quietly before Sikik noticed her.

Oolik was outside the minute Sikik left the next morning. Aqsuk had already roared away on his snowmobile. Oolik wouldn't come in when she saw some of Sikik's children and cousins still in the hut. Then Paniyapluk and the others motioned for her to come inside. They waved and smiled. They could hardly wait to see Oolik talk.

We repeated the signs we'd practiced. She could remember everything I'd shown her. Her fingers flew with language.

I wasn't exactly an expert, and Oolik's signs were sloppy. I even had to make up signs when I forgot something, but we were able to carry on conversations. I found out a lot about Oolik. She had no brothers or sisters. Her mother's babies had all died before they were a year old. Only Oolik had survived.

She told me kids had set fire to her clothes and pushed her down icy slopes. Boys had tried to drown her in the river.

"Oolik not stupid," she signed.

Sikik's children copied our motions. They, too, said "Oolik not stupid" with their hands, and that made Oolik smile.

It was a game, something to do. The kids practiced with one another, and then tried signing to Oolik. They laughed when she understood what they signed, nodded and signed back. You'd think Oolik had just stepped off a spaceship the way they all crowded around to ask her questions. I had to translate a lot or ask Oolik to repeat what she said with her hands. The kids kept asking how to say this and how to say that until I couldn't think straight.

"Me try, me try." The kids crowded close to face Oolik. One sat on my lap. Two hung over my shoulders. My head began to ache. I had meant to teach only Oolik to sign, not the whole village.

When Sikik and her neighbors came into the hut, they didn't chase Oolik away. They watched from a distance, arms folded above their stomachs, bandannas tied around their heads, feet spread apart.

"Ahhh. Deee!" Sikik said with a heavy sigh. "Oolik talk with hands now."

The women chuckled and shook their heads.

"I'm tired," I said with my hands. "Let's stop now."

Oolik's hands fell into her lap.

"Ahhh. Deee," Sikik said. She pressed her back and rocked back and forth from one foot to another. She grimaced. "Pain worse now. Baby come."

I'd never been around anyone who was about to deliver a baby, and I didn't know what I should do.

"Ahhh. Deee," Sikik said, sitting on the bed.

Some of her children gathered around her. Paniyapluk and a little sister tried to crawl onto her knees.

A woman shooed us from the hut. There wasn't any doctor to call, no hospital nearby. Sikik would have her baby at home.

We walked to John's store. There was a whole group of us, probably eight or ten kids besides Paniyapluk, Oolik, and me. Men had gathered there to talk and wait for the mail plane that never came.

No one seemed very concerned that Sikik was about to have her baby. Aqsuk seemed the least concerned of all. The men stood around the stove, warming their hands and talking in Iñupiat.

Then the signing started all over again, as Oolik pointed out things on the shelves. She grunted and pulled on my sleeve, dragging me from place to place.

"Look, Igri! Oolik talk now!" Paniyapluk said.

The men stopped talking to watch, amused smiles on their faces.

Paniyapluk stretched out her hands and sloppily signed to Oolik. Oolik answered.

"She talk with hands?" Aqsuk asked.

"Sign language," John said.

When she realized she was the center of attention, Oolik hid behind me.

"She make talk?" Aqsuk asked. "Some kinda joke maybe."

"It's not a joke," I said.

Aqsuk leaned against John's counter. "Talk, then," he said, folding his arms across his chest.

The men nodded. I had to pull Oolik from behind me. "They want you to talk," I signed. "Do you have something to say?"

Oolik's mouth twisted, and she covered her face with her hands.

John knelt down beside her, his hand on her shoulder. He took one of her hands in his and looked directly into her watery eye.

"Go on, Oolik," he said. "Don't be afraid."

Oolik was nervous, breathing hard, and trembling all over.

"It's all right," John said. "What do you want to say?"

Oolik held up a hand and signed. Even though the signs were carelessly done, I knew exactly what she meant to say.

"What she say?" Aqsuk asked.

Oolik looked up at me and made the signs again. She made them slowly and deliberately so I'd have no doubt about their meaning. She watched me closely, waiting for me to translate.

"Hey, Al . . . eee! What she say?" Aqsuk asked.

"She says, 'Eskimo stupid,' " I said.

Aqsuk straightened, jaws clenched. If he didn't hate me before, he sure hated me now.

"She say that?" he asked. "Why stupid?"

Oolik glared at Aqsuk and signed right in front of his face.

"What she say?" Aqsuk asked.

"She says, 'Our spirit dead,' " I said.

John had a curious look on his face, as if he'd just seen a falling star and didn't quite believe it. He looked over at Aqsuk with his mouth stretched tight. Then he stood up with a heavy sigh.

"What Oolik say?" Aqsuk asked.

"Too much whiskey," Oolik signed.

Again I translated.

"Too much talk. Too much sleep," Oolik said with her hands.

John stood close to Oolik. He placed a hand on Oolik's shoulder, and she leaned against his leg.

Aqsuk hunched his shoulders and stuffed a plug of tobacco along his jaw.

"I said it before and I'll say it again," John said. "We're going to die if we don't start taking responsibility for ourselves."

Aqsuk snarled. "What you want, Igri?" he asked. "You talk about old ways. This modern times now."

The men mumbled together, agreeing with Aqsuk. Matu and some of the boys entered the store and warmed themselves by the stove.

John nodded. "Kids are confused. I was confused, too, as a boy. I went to a mission school. Education destroyed my roots and my language. Now I don't belong anywhere. Not to this culture. Not to any other."

An old man stepped forward on bowed legs. "Iñupiat should be taught by Iñupiat," he said. "Not *Naluagmi*."

"We must listen to our village elders and keep the old ways as much as possible," John said. "But we must educate ourselves, too. We mustn't fall behind. One day we'll know the way."

Then he looked at me. "Right now, it's the *Naluagmi* who come and teach, and right now, it seems they offer us nothing."

10

THE GIFT

Bet you never see real Eskimo baby," Sikik said, cradling the newborn against her side. She lay on the bed, her dark hair moist against her cheek. I stepped closer. The baby was tiny, with an adorable, squeezed-together face and a shock of unruly blue-black hair that stuck out in every direction. My teddy bear was twice the size of Sikik's baby boy.

"Sikik want boy," she said. "Boy baby more better."

He was a perfect baby. Everyone in the village came to admire him. Every man, woman, and child got a turn holding him. Some rocked him in their arms. Some held him on their shoulders. Some kissed him on the belly. Everyone loved him.

Even Oolik's mother came. I'd never seen her before because she stayed apart from the rest of the village. She was husky-voiced and older than Sikik. Her faded parka dress was stained from Oolik's dirty hands, and the fur on her mukluks was matted. She must have been the poorest woman in the village. She had bags under her eyes and wore her hair in a long braid. Everything about her looked tired. She walked slowly, as if she ached all over. Oolik stayed behind her, watching every movement she made. The woman didn't gossip with the others or sit on the floor to sew muskrat skins. The hut grew so quiet while she was there that I could hear the bubbling water that boiled the moose nose on the stove. Sikik offered to let Oolik's mother hold the baby, and that was the only time the woman smiled.

Then Oolik and her mother left, going into the sweeping wind outside.

People hung around Sikik's hut, helping out. Some emptied the honeybuckets. Some scrubbed the dirty floor, getting down on their hands and knees and scouring it clean. Others played with the children, juggling stones with nut brown hands or twirling balls made out of scraps of fur. Sikik's hut was crowded with well-wishers.

They ate frozen fish dipped in smelly seal oil that someone had brought all the way from the coast. Their chins and fingers became shiny with grease. Women gave bites to their children before putting the oil-soaked fish into their own mouths.

An old woman promised me ice cream. She mixed melted fat and dried fish into seal oil, whipping it with her bare hand until it was foamy and smooth. Then she added cranberries and whipped it some more. When it became pink and creamy, I dipped a finger into the bowl. It was sour and reeked of oil. Only the old people ate it.

Women sang religious songs they'd learned from the time of the preacher. Men beat on drums made of skins stretched tight over hoops, and wailed monotonously while old people danced. It wasn't like any dance I'd ever seen, just a lot of shuffling and stomping of feet, but they seemed to be having a good time.

Sikik finally sent everyone out of the hut. Paniyapluk and her little sisters slept together under fur skins at the foot of her bed.

In spite of the wind, Matu went out with the boys to race snowmobiles on the river. After a while, some of Sikik's neighbors came back with their sewing. They sat on the floor with skins across their laps and sewed while Sikik slept. I felt like an outsider. I lay on my bedroll and watched from a corner.

The women talked, partly in English and partly in Iñupiat. They sewed, clucking their tongues. They warned Sikik that Aqsuk had gotten drunk on a brew he'd made from vanilla extract.

After everyone had gone home, Aqsuk came charging in. Sikik shooed him outside because most of the kids were sleeping. He stomped his feet and cursed. I heard him start up his snowmobile. Then he roared around the village, keeping everyone awake most of the night.

I didn't hear him come home, but he was there in the morning, vomiting in a bucket. He had frostbite on the high points of his cheeks. He spoke roughly to Sikik and slammed the doors as he stomped out. His snowmobile wouldn't work.

Even though they had worked perfectly well the night before, eight other snowmobiles were inoperable, too. The angry men huddled outside the hut with Aqsuk to consider the problem, then they walked down to John's store.

By the time Oolik came for lessons, Sikik's friends were already there. They watched us and tried to imitate our signs.

"What Oolik say now?" Sikik asked every time Oolik made a sign.

"What you say to Oolik?" she asked every time I signed back.

I had to repeat every sign I made until the women nodded with understanding. They were as curious as the children and just as anxious to learn. They didn't want to be left out of any conversation.

Then Oolik made a confession. I didn't know whether to translate or not, but the women insisted. Oolik had put sugar in the snowmobile fuel tanks.

The women shrieked with laughter.

"Ah! Dee! Now men take machines apart," Sikik said, laughing. "Quiet tonight maybe."

The other women laughed, too. They said it was the best thing Oolik could have done.

I didn't have anything to give the new baby, so I gave him my teddy bear. It was old, the golden fur worn smooth, but the black button eyes were still shiny and sewn tight. Sikik laughed when I handed it to her.

"Only cloth bear," she said.

"He'll like it when he gets bigger," I said. "I've had it since I was three years old."

She tossed the bear onto the bed.

It was a big sacrifice to give away my childhood friend. Paniyapluk and the other kids didn't have toys to play with, not real toys like electric trains and dolls. They played with whatever was around, a big spoon or bits of fur or mukluk lacings.

Matu and the bigger boys shot baskets with a mail-order ball through a hoop attached to the side of Sikik's hut. Over and over, they shot the basketball through the hoop. It bounced on Sikik's hut with a loud, rhythmic *thump, thump, thump.*

Sikik was in good spirits. She'd been happy ever since the birth of her baby and was up and around in no time, stirring the soup on the stove or writing her mail orders. She was very popular because she'd had a boy baby.

Then she announced, "Sikik give baby to Oolik's hut."

Everyone looked at her. It was so silent in the room, I could hear the wind blowing outside. Oolik stood with a puzzled expression on her face because Sikik was smiling at her, but hadn't signed. The women left their sewing and came to gather around Oolik.

"Tell Oolik," Sikik said. She waited, then nudged me. "Oolik's mama adopt this baby."

I thought she was joking, but I signed.

Oolik frowned, and I signed again. A smile spread across her face. She made some signs that meant "so happy! so happy!"

My heart sank. It was a cruel joke. The women circled like blackbirds, heads bobbing up and down as they clucked and chattered. Suddenly, I realized they were not laughing at Oolik. Sikik had not been joking.

"Hey, wait a minute!" I said. "You can't just give your baby away!"

Sikik's smile faded. "This *good* baby!" she said.

"But he's *your* baby," I said.

"Oolik's hut need baby," Sikik said. "Oolik's hut need boy baby."

"But you're his mother!" I said.

"Baby got new mama now," one of the women said.

Sikik turned her back on me to whisper behind her hand to her friends.

My head throbbed. I sat on the floor against the wall and buried my face in my hands.

Paniyapluk leaned against me to watch me cry, and I felt the tug of Oolik's hands and heard that familiar deep grunting sound she made to get my attention. I was sick of Oolik and her signing.

She pulled on my hair, making me raise my head. Then she signed in front of my face.

"Why Al . . . eee cry?" she asked.

She was so close I could smell her. Her long misshapen eye was examining my face closely.

I tried to explain how I felt about Sikik giving the baby away, but Oolik didn't understand. She went home. Matu came in after feeding the dogs and lounged around on the floor with some of the older kids.

"Sikik's giving the baby away," I said.

"That so?" Matu replied.

"To Oolik's mother!"

It didn't matter one bit to him. "Sikik already got babies maybe," he said.

"A mother can't just give her baby away."

"Oolik's mother have only Oolik," he said.

The women were passing the baby around. They took turns patting him on the back and rocking him in their arms. Then they handed the baby over to the kids, and they each had a turn. There wasn't a minute when the baby wasn't held. He seemed perfectly content, dozing even while he was being jostled and admired.

"Baby grow big," Matu said. "Raise dogs. Hunt caribou. Trap muskrat. Oolik's hut not go hungry now."

Sikik looked over and smiled at Matu.

Even though it stormed the next day, Oolik's mother came and took the baby to her hut. Sikik wasn't criticized and did not lose her popularity.

11

CRAZY ANUN

Sikik's hut seemed empty after the baby was gone, but Sikik didn't seem to mind. In spite of the windstorm that swept snow into creamy piles, Oolik's mother returned several times a day for Sikik to nurse the baby. Sometimes Sikik walked up to Oolik's hut.

Something changed in the village. Oolik wasn't exactly accepted by everyone, but she was no longer ostracized. People went to her hut to see the baby. It was as if the baby belonged to everyone. Women continued to gather in Sikik's hut to sew, but they met in Oolik's hut, too.

Outside John's store the men watched me curiously. They murmured together, pointing me out.

"They say you gave Oolik a sign," John said. "That's what brought about the happiness in Oolik's hut."

"What do you mean?"

"Oolik can make herself understood now," John said. "She never tried before. Everyone treated her badly. You were kind enough to teach her about signing, and that's made a difference."

"I hope you don't mean Sikik gave the baby away because Oolik can sign."

"Well, I guess that's exactly what I mean. Sikik sees Oolik differently now. We all do. That means Oolik's mother is looked at differently, too."

He was tinkering with his radio. "By the way, Search and Rescue found your plane. I got my radio to work long enough to hear that much. We'll find out what village your mother is in, and we'll get you there on the next plane out."

"That's a relief," I said. Then I asked, "How can you live in such a far away, isolated place?"

"Most of the villages cropped up in places where our ancestors had fish camps," he said. "This village has been here two thousand years."

Aqsuk came into the store and asked John for vanilla extract.

"I'm just about to close," John said. "And you know I won't sell you that stuff. I won't even put it out on the shelves. Understand?"

Aqsuk cussed, and brushed by me so fast he almost knocked me over. He pushed past John, heading for the back room where John stored some of his supplies. I could hear one of John's kids crying beyond the curtain that was the doorway into John's home. I could smell caribou soup and hear the soft, low tones of John's wife as she talked with a neighbor.

"Go home, Aqsuk!" John said. "Sober up."

Aqsuk swayed only inches from me. I stepped back out of the way. He doubled his fists and swung. John caught his arm, holding it high.

"Better run along, Allison," he said. "Go on, get out of here."

I backed out the door.

John held Aqsuk by his parka ruff. He shoved him outside where I stood. Then he bolted the door. I heard the iron bolt fall into place.

All the way back to the hut, I could hear Aqsuk shouting and banging on the door with his fists.

I didn't say anything to Sikik. We settled down in our usual places on the floor. I sat on my bedroll, not ready for sleep. I was so anxious to talk to someone I wrote another letter to Mom.

"Dear Mom,

Please come get me if you can. I know I was a brat sometimes. I admit my grades went down in math and science, but they were still good in English. Even though I couldn't get to the clinic every day, I still managed to go on Saturdays.

Everything was different in Dana Point. You weren't there, and Dad didn't have much time. When I came here, I was hoping we could all move back to Huntington Beach and be a normal family again. That house is gone, sold! Everyone here is part of a family. Everyone except me.

There's a deaf girl here. Her name is Oolik.

I miss you. I want to go home.

Your long lost daughter, Allison"

I shoved the journal back into my duffel and crawled into my bedroll. There were a lot of things I wanted to talk to Mom about. She'd tell me how a mother could give her baby away and how to deal with Aqsuk.

The family was asleep, and Sikik was getting ready for bed when Aqsuk came storming into the hut.

He wobbled as he walked, and his eyes were pinched and watery. He made so much noise as he entered, that he woke the children.

"Paniyapluk! Come!" he said. The smallest children sat on Sikik's bed, their arms wrapped around each other. Paniyapluk had been dozing on fur skins not far from me. She sat up, rubbing her eyes, and I sat up, too. "Paniyapluk! Come!" He motioned for her to follow him outside.

Paniyapluk looked at Sikik, then at me. She shook her head, her black hair gleaming in the dim light.

Sikik came over and planted herself right in front of Paniyapluk, partially hiding her from Aqsuk's view.

"Paniyapluk stay," she said, folding her arms in front of her chest and spreading her legs.

Aqsuk cussed, his voice low and husky. He stepped forward, swaying a little. Then he raised a hand and struck Sikik right in the face. Blood ran from her nose.

She hardly even flinched. She stood there, her arms folded across her chest, her feet spread apart, watching Aqsuk as blood rolled down her face.

Aqsuk looked at his hand as if it didn't belong to him. Then he made a fist and struck Sikik again. I could hear the sound of his knuckles cracking against her cheekbone.

The next time, Sikik was ready. She put her hands in front of her face, but she did not move from her position. It was as if her feet were stuck to the floor.

Aqsuk raised his fist and struck again. Blood oozed

from the center of the purple bruise on Sikik's cheek. Aqsuk stepped closer, both fists doubled.

"Stop!" I shouted.

Aqsuk paused, fists in front of him like a boxer, swaying side to side.

Sikik didn't fight back. She just stood, moaning and sort of rocking back and forth. "Ah! Deee! Ah! Deee! Stupid *anun*."

I hoped Matu or some of Sikik's older boys would come into the hut. I tried to make myself small inside my bedroll.

"Paniyapluk! Come!" Aqsuk said again.

"No!" Paniyapluk said. She folded her arms in front of her.

To my surprise, Aqsuk turned around and stomped out of the hut.

"Ahhh! Deee!" Sikik said, sinking onto the bed with a weary sigh. She dabbed at her wounds with a flowered bandanna and brushed blood from her clothing as if it were nothing more than snow.

I brought her a cup of water from the barrel. She dipped the bandanna into the water and held it to her face. I was shaking so much, water sloshed on the floor.

I could hear Aqsuk start up a neighbor's snowmobile, one of the few not ruined by Oolik's sugar. He roared around the village, gunning the motor as he wound between the huts. He headed up to the cemetery knoll and circled around, then plunged down the steep slope to the river.

The noise started Matu's dogs barking. Dogs on the other side of the village joined the chorus. Wolves howled somewhere in the distance. Aqsuk traveled the same route over and over, going faster and faster, gunning his engine every time he passed Sikik's hut. If only Matu would come back!

I peered outside the tiny window and could see Aqsuk's angry silhouette in the moonlight. The village huts were black. There was only a faint orange light in the store by the river. Again, I heard the roaring snowmobile. Again and again.

Then I heard shots. They sounded like firecrackers. *Pop! Pop! Pop!* Sikik's face twisted. Paniyapluk shook all over and put her arms around her little sister.

"Crazy *anun!*" Sikik said. "Aqsuk stupid man."

There was another shot, this time close to Sikik's hut. The dogs yelped and squealed.

Matu burst into the hut, powdery snow falling from his boots. "Aqsuk shoot Amaguq!"

Sikik rushed to the door, surrounded by a half-dozen children. I followed them through the cunnychuck. Matu's lead dog lay dead upon the snow, eyes as hard as marbles. The rest of the dogs strained against their chains, yelping and whining.

Matu hurried toward the river carrying his gun. All the boys in the village seemed to be right behind him, and they carried guns, too. They disappeared into the darkness, their shouts making the swirling green veils of light spin and soar against the black sky.

Men in neighboring huts jumped on the nearest snowmobiles that were operational and raced down the slope toward the river.

"Ahhh! Deee!" Sikik moaned, shooing us back inside the hut.

When we couldn't hear the snowmobiles anymore or the shouts of the boys, and when the dogs ceased barking and there was only the distant howling of the wolves and the wind, the children fell asleep.

I hid deep inside my bedroll, praying that Matu wouldn't shoot Aqsuk and hoping Aqsuk wouldn't come back to the hut. I just wanted everything to be normal again, even though I'd never thought of life in Sikik's village as particularly normal.

"Matu should have stayed home," I said to Sikik over the sleeping children.

"Matu man now," Sikik said. "*Naluagmi* not tell him what to do."

She sewed, sitting on the floor and rocking back and forth. "Ahhh! Deee!" Now and then she touched her wounded face. Then she cussed in Iñupiat, the strange words spitting and harsh. She sat facing the door as if to guard Paniyapluk and the rest of us from Aqsuk.

When she finally lay on her bed with a heavy sigh, I fell asleep.

I was dreaming of Oolik. I could hear the thump of her foot and the scrape of the stiff hide sole of her mukluk as she dragged herself across the floor. Then there was the usual pause as she used that leg as a crutch to vault forward.

She stretched out her hands and reached for me, clutching my shirt. My eyes flew open and she was there, her face twisting with the agony of her speechlessness.

Strange sounds came from her throat. I sat up, realizing I wasn't dreaming. Matu and the boys hadn't returned. There were no snowmobiles roaring outside, but something was wrong, something acrid in the air. Sikik and the children were sleeping soundly. No one had awakened when Oolik entered the hut. The thought disturbed me because Aqsuk could have entered just as easily.

"What is it?" I asked, frowning. "Is it Matu?"

Oolik made some signs, her fingers flying so fast in the darkness that I couldn't grasp what she was saying. She waited, and when I didn't respond, she repeated the signs slower this time. Then I understood.

"Sikik! Fire! The store!"

Sikik immediately rose from the cluster of children and pulled on her clothes. I struggled into my thermal socks and boots, wrapped the long woolen scarf across my face, then got my parka, cap, and mittens.

Sikik was bundled and already at the door, tying a bandanna under her chin.

Oolik dragged herself after Sikik.

Paniyapluk and the other children were scrambling into their heavy outerwear, their huge beaver mittens attached to braided strands of colored yarn that hung around their necks.

Even from Sikik's hut, we could see the blaze, bright and orange. People ran from all directions, carrying buckets and yelling. The sounds echoed in the icy blackness. *Crackle! Sizzle!* There was the pop of tin and aluminum, the explosion of ammunition.

There were no emergency vehicles, no 9-1-1, no fire

department or sirens sending out an alarm. Worst of all, there was no running water.

Matu and the boys were nowhere in sight. The men who usually hung around John's store were gone, too. And so was John.

Bundled women and village elders rapidly crossed the icy slope toward the leaping flames. John's wife and three children were wrapped in furs, the glow of the flames casting shadows across their faces.

Children ran to the river, carrying buckets. They pulled up the long poles that marked their water holes and broke through the new skin of ice. Everyone formed a human chain that led from the fire to the river. Buckets were passed from one to another, water slopping over the rims and spilling to the ground. People standing closest to the blaze threw the water. Someone handed me a bucket filled with ice-cold river water, and I passed it along. We moved quickly, as quickly as we could, and no one pushed or shoved or shouted orders. Everyone knew what had to be done.

It was hopeless. The fire was too big, and it took too long to get water out of the small holes in the ice. Sikik, Oolik, and some of the women shoveled snow onto the flames, but it was no use.

Finally, everyone dropped the buckets and watched the fire burn itself out. In the end, there was nothing left but smoking timbers.

"How did it start?" I asked.

No one seemed to know.

"Was it the oil stove?" I asked.

No one answered.

John's wife and children went to stay with a village elder. As people headed back to their homes, Oolik pulled me aside.

She made the sign for "drunk," her thumb tilted toward her mouth. She reached up for the imaginary cap brim, meaning "man." Then she made the sign for fire.

"Drunken man set fire?" I asked.

"I see him. He saw me," she signed.

"Aqsuk?" I made the sign for man and pointed to Sikik's back.

She nodded. Her fingers said more. She'd seen him light matches and throw them through a damaged window before jumping back on the snowmobile. She thought the matches had gone out. A long time passed before there were flames. By then, the men were long gone, chasing Aqsuk on the river.

She put her fingers to her lips, signing "secret."

I signed "secret for now."

She looked at me, her huge misshapen eye filled with fear, and I understood. If Aqsuk had seen her, he would shoot her or run over her with a snowmobile or bury her in snow.

I watched her struggle up the icy slope toward her hut.

I'd promised Oolik I'd say nothing to Sikik. I didn't sleep a wink the rest of the night. I held Oolik's secret in my mind, imagining over and over how Aqsuk had destroyed John's place. I listened to Sikik snoring and the children sighing in their sleep. I'd tell only Matu. He'd know what to do. I waited, but Matu and the boys didn't come home. I heard the dogs barking and jiggling their chains.

When I woke up, it was strangely quiet. Sikik arose and went outside to the food cache to get caribou for soup.

She came in with the frozen meat under her arm, saying, "Ahhh! Deee! Matu and boys gone too long maybe."

Paniyapluk and I went outside to wait. Snow was falling, covering the oil barrels and broken snowmobiles and piles of antlers.

"Dogs gone," Paniyapluk said, pointing to the stakes where Matu kept his dogs.

I looked at the spot where the dogs had been. I hadn't heard Matu come back to get them.

Their chains lay limply on the packed, stained ice. Only Amaguq remained behind, rigid and dusted by the falling snow.

12

BLUE TICKET

In the soft spread of sunrise, I saw Matu standing at the rear of his sled as the wildly yelping dogs bolted across the frozen river. They approached the village, zigzagging more than usual, not as rhythmic as before, bouncing and darting like confused puppies without Amaguq.

Sikik and her neighbors stood outside their huts, flowered bandannas tied around their heads to keep the cold air from their ears.

We waited as Matu and the dogs got nearer. They were going slowly. In the distance, we could see some of the boys running after Matu.

The dogs came up to Sikik's house. Aqsuk was in the sled, his face twisted with pain.

No one scolded or questioned Matu for being gone such a long time. The women waited, hands hidden inside their deep pockets, their eyes squeezing into quarter moons.

Aqsuk struggled to get out of the sled. He stood on one

leg, groaning in agony, and held an arm close to his body as if it were a heavy log. The boys half carried, half dragged him into the hut.

His arm must have been broken, and his ankle was swollen about three times its normal size. The snowmobile had fallen on top of him when he'd gone up an incline that was too steep. The women shook their heads, saying it was a wonder such a "stupid *anun*" wasn't killed.

John had sent Matu back on foot for the sled. It was the only way to get Aqsuk home because, one by one, the snowmobiles had run out of fuel. The men built shelters out of blocks of ice. They camped and in the early hours loaded Aqsuk onto the sled. Abandoning their snowmobiles, they trudged home on the river.

Sikik wrung her hands and paced the floor. "Ahhh! Deee!" she sighed. "Crazy *anun*. Stupid *anun*, drink too much."

Aqsuk lay on the bed, moaning. He hollered as Sikik and her neighbors held him and pulled his arm. Sikik bound the arm tightly with strips of cloth.

"He should have that arm X-rayed," I said.

I knew about broken bones. I'd fallen off the monkey bars at school during recess when I was in kindergarten and had broken my arm. Mom said that compound fractures had to be set properly.

Everyone ignored me because John and some of the men, their parkas coated with snow, came into Sikik's hut speaking excitedly in Iñupiat. Everyone was talking at once. More people crowded into the hut, including John's wife and children. Even Oolik, her mother, and the new baby they called Putu were there. They talked on and on about the fire.

John said something must have fallen against the stove.

Sikik's children played noisily, expecting to get the attention of the adults, but no one picked them up or tossed them in the air.

Matu stood beside Aqsuk, his arms folded across his chest. "Dogs need Amaguq!" he said. "Amaguq dead!"

Aqsuk looked away and moaned.

John put a hand on Matu's shoulder. "A stray bullet must have hit your dog while Aqsuk was shooting up the village. It was an unfortunate accident."

Matu shook John's hand off his shoulder. "Aqsuk shoot on purpose maybe," he said. "Village should blue-ticket Aqsuk."

The women whispered together.

"Even without Amaguq, your team managed all right," John said. "Choose one of the others to take his place."

"Matu only lost dog," Sikik said, scolding her nephew. "Igri lost store. Whole village lost store."

Aqsuk's narrow eyes narrowed even more. He looked at his neighbors, at the men standing nearby, and at the women tending to his injuries. Then his eyes rested on Oolik.

She didn't flinch. She stared right back at him with her uneven eyes and squared her crooked shoulders.

Aqsuk's eyes searched back and forth between Oolik's good eye and the huge lopsided eye. Hatred spread across his face and his mouth formed a sneer.

Oolik held her hands up and rapidly made some signs.

She was speaking directly to Aqsuk, and it was as if her fingers could hiss and spit. Only a deaf girl had seen Aqsuk set fire to John's store, a deaf girl who had never before been able to communicate. And now, even someone who knew nothing about signing would know that Oolik was accusing him of something more than shooting Matu's dog.

All eyes turned to me. I didn't say a word. Oolik made the signs again, this time right in front of my face. Everyone waited, especially Oolik.

"What Oolik say?" Matu asked.

"Aqsuk set the fire," I said. "Oolik saw him do it."

I expected everyone to start shouting at Aqsuk. I thought they'd throw him off the bed and kick him out of the house.

Instead, they were silent, staring at me in disbelief. Even John said nothing.

Sikik clucked her tongue. Some of the women whispered together behind their hands. Paniyapluk doubled up a fist and struck me in the stomach.

"*Sugloo!*" she shouted. "Al . . . eee *sugloo!*"

I couldn't believe what was happening.

Paniyapluk ran over to Oolik and knocked her down onto the floor, striking her over and over with her fists. "Oolik *sugloo! Sugloo!*"

No one stopped her.

I looked at Matu for help.

"They think white girl lie maybe," he said.

Oolik and I were alone against the others. No one could believe such an awful thing of a neighbor. No one thought Aqsuk would deliberately set fire to John's house and burn down the only village store.

"Oolik is telling the truth," I said.

Sikik stared directly at me, her lips a snarl. "Al . . . eee *sugloo*," she said.

John put a hand on my shoulder. "Perhaps you're mistaken," he said. "Oolik is only learning to sign. Perhaps that's not what Oolik is saying at all."

"Oolik only crippled girl," Aqsuk said.

I could feel Oolik's eyes on me as I glared at Aqsuk.

Suddenly, there was a noise outside, and the dogs started barking wildly. I could hear the whoosh of sled runners on the snow.

"Ikayauq come!" Matu said.

Everyone left Aqsuk and ran outside. The barking became joyous as the older dogs greeted Matu's yelping, squealing pups.

"Wolverine!" Ikayauq said, grinning.

Matu was grinning, too, no longer concerned about Amaguq or Aqsuk. "Wolverine clever," he explained. "Hunter in past life."

Ikayauq hung the animal upside down in Sikik's cunnychuck, the nose pointing to the floor, the tail near the ceiling, the huge body covered with long black and white fur that would make many fine parka ruffs.

The wolverine seemed to help everyone forget about the fire.

I couldn't forget. It was as if someone had died and no one was talking about it. I had this heavy, depressed feeling I couldn't shake. I hated having Aqsuk in the hut. I wanted to leave more than ever. "Now maybe we can go to the coast," I said to Matu.

"I go back with Ikayauq tomorrow," he said.

Matu and Ikayauq talked in Iñupiat, making plans for the trail. Their plans obviously didn't include me.

When Matu woke me early in the morning, he was already dressed in fur for the trail, and an icy breeze surrounded him. "Come!" he said. "See Oolik!"

I dressed quickly and followed him outside. Oolik was in Matu's sled, her belongings beside her. She signed rapidly with her fingers, demanding that Matu take her to the coast.

"Oolik! Out!" Matu said, motioning for her to move.

Oolik refused to budge. "Oolik blue-ticket Oolik! I go to school!" she signed, then she crossed her arms in front of her chest.

I translated for Matu.

"Stupid girl want to go to school on coast," Matu said. "Too bad Matu going back with Ikayauq." He shook his head and laughed. "Oolik sit in sled 'til breakup, maybe sit forever!"

He tossed her pathetic duffel into a swirl of snow. Oolik stared straight ahead, her stubborn jaw doubling up like a fist.

13

MISSING PERSON

Oolik dragged herself and her duffel to her usual watching place.

John came hurrying up the slope, waving an arm and shouting. I thought he'd come to say good-bye to Ikayauq and Matu.

"We need your sleds," he shouted. He spoke in English and then in Iñupiat, turning from one to the other. "We must take fuel out to the snowmobiles so we can get them back."

Ikayauq wrinkled his nose and stared stonily off into the distance.

"It's too far to walk carrying fuel," John said. "We can't just leave all those machines out there."

Ikayauq rubbed his chin thoughtfully. He was studying Matu and smiling slowly, but he said nothing.

"Too much work!" Matu said. "Sleds already loaded."

"Look, Matu, we need you," John said. "There's not a single dog team left in this village, not anymore."

"You got dogs," Matu said.

"Sure, we've got lots of dogs, but none are trained as a team."

Ikayauq pursed his lips, then looked down at the trampled snow. He said something in Iñupiat, then chuckled.

"I know," John said. "I'm as much to blame as anyone. I've made money on every snowmobile ordered through my store. I've made money on the cola we drink and on the jawbreakers that rot our teeth."

Ikayauq clucked his tongue and spoke rapidly in Iñupiat. The words were harsh and scolding.

"Ikayauq says men should raise dogs," Matu said. "Fuel not last forever."

"Will you help?" John said.

"Too many men," Matu said. "Two sleds not enough."

"The boys will go," John said. "They don't weigh as much as men."

Matu looked over at me. "Girl lighter than boy maybe," he said.

"Will you go along, Allison?" John asked. "Help bring a snowmobile back?"

"Well, sure, I guess so," I said.

"The weather's good, at least for now."

Matu and Ikayauq quickly unloaded their sleds. Matu heaped everything on the snow. Ikayauq carefully stacked his things—the equipment for the trail, the traps, and the dead animals. All the time, he was chuckling to himself and shaking his head.

I rode in Ikayauq's sled with some boys and drums of fuel.

Matu took his cousins and even more fuel.

The sky was clear, as daylight spread pink and gold across the ice. The two teams raced on the river, sometimes Ikayauq ahead, sometimes Matu.

Everyone chattered with excitement, but I was probably the most excited of all to be traveling away from the village. The seasons had changed. The days were longer.

The boys gazed off into the distance. There was nothing to see but snow and ice and clumps of small, straggly trees.

I needed to use the bathroom, and there wasn't any place to go in all that wilderness, not even the horrid honeybucket Sikik had in her hut. When I couldn't wait any longer, I asked Ikayauq to stop. After a long while, Ikayauq stopped his dogs. Matu came up alongside, his dogs yelping. It was really embarrassing because the boys were snickering as I climbed the riverbank toward a clump of trees.

Right in the middle of everything, with my overalls unzipped and my parka off, there was a sudden, startling animal sound right behind me. I nearly jumped out of my skin. I whirled around to face the biggest, ugliest deer I'd ever seen. It was bigger than a horse and had a large antler rack. It stared at me for a minute, snorting, then lowered its head and charged.

I screamed and ran like crazy for the river, yelling at the top of my lungs, clutching the straps of my overalls, and dragging my parka behind me.

"Help! Help!" My throat burned from gulping icy air. Still in their traces, the dogs went mad, jumping and howling.

"Moose!" someone shouted. "Al . . . eee found moose!"

Whooping, the boys grabbed their guns.

I tripped and fell facedown in the snow as a volley of shots rang overhead. I lay still, gasping and listening to the pounding of my heart and the baying of the dogs.

Ikayauq and the boys knew just what to do. They slit the animal's throat and sliced the underbelly. Then they cut around the hooves and up the legs. Pulling and cutting, they slipped the hide away from the carcass. Soon there was a bloody mess all over the snow. Ikayauq and the boys were covered with blood, and they were joking about me.

"Al . . . eee pee and find moose!"

According to Ikayauq, who knew about such things, the moose was a sign of good luck.

I sat on his sled, watching the sharp knives cut through sinew and bone. I'd never seen anything like it in my life. I threw up on the snow, and everyone was too busy butchering to notice.

Matu tossed small bits of meat to the dogs to keep them from barking so wildly. Even before my stomach felt normal, we were on the trail, both sleds loaded with not only boys and fuel but also moose meat.

The abandoned snowmobiles were spread out over a long distance. We dropped off fuel and a driver at each machine. Snow had to be scooped off the seats before they could be ridden. One by one, the boys fueled and started up the machines.

Finally, it was my turn.

I'd ridden on a motorcycle once when Dad was thinking about buying one. He'd driven out of the parking lot with me on the back—a test drive—and he gunned the engine and made a turn that was too sharp. We crashed. Mom said it was a miracle we weren't hurt, and that only Dad's pride was injured. Dad decided not to get a motorcycle, and he bought a supercharged Porsche instead.

I straddled the wide seat, anxious to catch up with the boys. Ikayauq and Matu turned their teams around while I squeezed the throttle. The snowmobile took off too fast. I immediately hit a bumpy spot on the ice. The snowmobile spun and turned, spilling me on the ground.

Matu burst out laughing. "Al . . . eee never ride snowmobile maybe," he said.

I struggled to my feet, brushing snow off my clothes. I lived in southern California. How did he expect me to know how to drive a snowmobile?

Matu came over to help me get the snowmobile back into position. Then he spread his hands and leaned from side to side, showing me how to balance as I steered.

I boarded again, trembling as I started off slowly. The boys were far down the river and almost out of sight. Ikayauq was long gone. Matu waited, watching, edging his team slowly down the river not far from me.

After a while, I got the hang of it. I leaned right, then left, anticipating the bumps and ridges on the ice. Before long, I was soaring across the ice, laughing until my face ached.

Matu's sled slid over the river, his dogs racing, but he never went too far ahead of me and never dropped too far behind.

As I came close to the village, I could see a group of

people circling a towering stack of cola, crates of canned goods, and at least three dozen cardboard boxes filled with supplies.

"Mail plane come!" Matu shouted.

I stopped the snowmobile to watch people load the things onto Matu's sled. John was directing the supplies to the abandoned schoolhouse that would be his new store. There were cartons of cigarettes, rifles, packages addressed to Sikik and Aqsuk and others in the village, and a duffel bag stuffed with letters. The supplies had been ordered weeks, maybe months before.

I couldn't believe my luck! The mail plane had finally come, and it had gone!

John saw me and hurried over.

"You'll be heading home tomorrow," he said. "The plane will be back in the morning with more supplies."

"Why didn't you tell the plane to wait? I could have flown out today."

"A lot of villages have been waiting for mail," he said. "You aren't top priority around here."

Matu straightened, his eyes meeting mine. "Aqsuk top priority today maybe," he said.

"Aqsuk? Is he going to a hospital?" I asked.

John and Matu exchanged glances.

"The village council voted him out of the village," John said.

"Elders hear Oolik, maybe," Matu said.

14

HOME

I went up the slope to Oolik. She was in the very spot where I'd first seen her. We stood there, side by side, two village outcasts.

"I'm going home," I said, making the signs for "eat" and "sleep."

Oolik watched closely. I put the closed fingers of my right hand to my lips. Then I placed a flat palm against my right cheek as if resting my head on a pillow.

Eat. Sleep. Home.

Oolik pointed to me and imitated the signs. Then she put her fingertips to her lips as if tasting something and pulled her hand into a thumbs-up position. Better. "Is your home better?" she'd asked.

Home had once meant so many things to me. Mom. Dad. My own room. My posters and horse shelf and clothes. My things. I'd never thought about home being mainly a place to eat and sleep.

Sikik's hut was always warm and cozy with chattering children and caribou soup simmering on the stove, a place to eat and sleep. It was home.

Oolik smiled her lopsided smile.

She signed that my home was better. She had a mother and a new baby brother, but that wasn't enough for Oolik.

I placed my fingertips to my forehead, then moved my hand down into the Y position. "Why?" I asked.

Oolik clapped her hands together several times. "School."

My home was better. My home had a school. Oolik was the only child in the village who was anxious to go to school.

"Oolik learn," she signed. "Oolik teach."

She held her hands open, facing each other, and moved them up and down.

"Someday," I said. "Maybe." She tugged on my arm. "I must get ready to go," I said, but I didn't sign. I hurried to Sikik's hut.

Aqsuk was gone, blue-ticketed somewhere, but there were reminders of him in the hut—his tobacco, a wrinkled shirt, a knitted headband. I went through the motions of getting ready to go. I gave my tube of posters and silly white boots to Paniyapluk.

I was too excited to sleep, and lay shivering inside my bedroll listening to Sikik's steady snoring.

I heard the plane buzz the village early the next morning. It circled overhead several times before landing on the river. It came down like a giant metal bird. Everyone hurried down to the river: women in flowered bandannas, children bundled in fur, men in fancy mukluks. I carried my duffel to the river and stood with it near my feet.

I was scared to death.

The last thing in the world I wanted to do was get on that plane and go to another strange, new place all by myself. I could feel tears press behind my eyes as I thought of Oolik and Paniyapluk and Matu. They were my only friends, and I was leaving them behind.

When I turned to look back at the village, I saw Oolik dragging herself down the slope. Matu was walking behind, overtaking her. Oolik paused and looked up at him, bracing herself. Matu nodded to her, then signed something. Oolik signed back. Matu slowed his pace to walk beside her.

Then Oolik saw me watching. I put my fingertips to my mouth, then moved my hand away, palm up, saying "thank you."

She stood rigidly, unsmiling. We stared at one another for a long time. Finally, as I was about to turn away, she put her fingertips to her mouth and moved her hand away, palm up. It was good-bye.

There was a commotion as several people jumped from the plane and started handing down boxes.

"Allison!"

My heart skipped a beat. I tried to see who had called. Only her voice was familiar. Gone was the perfect hair. Straggly wisps stuck out below the woolen cap like feathers. The impostor waved her arms and smiled, but I couldn't move from the spot. All I could do was stare.

"Allison! It's me! It's Mom!"

There was something familiar in her eyes.

She seemed older. A web of lines had grown around

her eyes. But she seemed younger, too. She moved like a boy, her huge bunny boots smacking onto the ice as if it was something she did every day. She wrapped her arms around me.

"Mom! You came!"

"I found you at last," she said. She shook me a little. "That's *you* in there, isn't it?" Mom asked.

She was my mother all right.

"Do I look that bad?" I asked.

She laughed. It was a brittle, husky sound. "I guess we've both looked better," she said. "Good God, Allison, you could have been killed! Your Dad will never forgive me. I'll never forgive myself." She was laughing and crying at the same time.

"Gosh, Mom, you look different," I said.

"Life's hard enough, but life in the Arctic is especially harsh," she said. "You've changed, too, honey. You've grown. You're taller than I am."

She touched my face with a fuzzy mitten and wiped away a tear before it froze on my cheek.

She caught me in her arms, and I hugged her as tightly as I could. Then we watched the men unload the plane.

Paniyapluk stared rudely at Mom, then turned and signed something to Oolik. Sikik and her neighbors whispered behind their hands. Matu and Ikayauq had already repacked their sleds and were ready for the trail.

Ikayauq stepped onto the back runner and shouted a command. Then, with a whooshing sound, his team left all of us behind. I watched him get smaller and smaller as his dogs raced across the river.

"That was the man who saved my life," I said.

"My goodness, why didn't you say so?" Mom said. "I would like to thank him or give him a reward or something."

"He doesn't need anything," I said.

Matu stepped onto the runner behind his sled and took off after Ikayauq. His dogs zigzagged back and forth, loping along lazily. As he slid toward the river, he raised an arm, and I waved.

Mom was studying the people standing on the riverbank. "Who's that child?" she asked, staring at Oolik, who was signing to Paniyapluk and some of the other children. "My goodness, are *all* those children deaf?"

"Only Oolik," I said.

"She must have a difficult time in all this snow and ice."

"She does all right," I said.

Mom watched Oolik move up the slope, dragging her leg, then vaulting forward. Some of the children followed her.

"She certainly seems popular enough," Mom said.

The pilot motioned that it was time to go.

"I have to say good-bye to Sikik, to thank her for everything."

"Oh, my goodness, yes. Hurry!"

"Make sure the plane doesn't leave without me."

Sikik was tossing the contents of a slop bucket onto the snow. The dirty water froze instantly upon the rainbow of earlier spillings.

"I'm going now," I said.

She nodded but didn't look at me.

"Well, good-bye, Sikik, and thank you for everything."
She nodded again. "And say good-bye to all the kids,
okay?"

She still hadn't looked at me, so I turned to go. Then
she caught my hand with both of hers, and even through
my mittens, I could feel how warm they were. We faced
each other, and her eyes were twinkling.

"Iñupiat on coast might like white girl, maybe," she
said. It was the best thing she could have said to me.

I hurried to where Mom was waiting. We walked down
the slope and out onto the frozen river.

"Our quarters were built by the Bureau of Indian
Affairs years ago," Mom said. "The school's on one side. It's
nothing much, sort of a duplex. I hope you won't be too
disappointed. "

"It's OK, Mom." I said.

We boarded the plane. When we were above the village, I could see what remained of John's store, black
timbers jutting out of the snow. I looked for Sikik's hut,
but the plane lifted and turned northwest.

"When I first came here, they seemed strange," I said.
"Now they're just regular people."

She laughed. "You mean, like people back home?"

"Well, no. Better than that. Stronger. Self-reliant. I
hope they don't change."

"What do you mean?" she asked. "They must change if
they're ever going to join this century."

"Why do they have to be like us?" I asked.

"Honey, they're in a confusing stage right now, one
foot in the old world, the other in the new."

"It sure changes things," I said.

"What does?"

"Us coming here."

"I know," she said. "It changes us. It changes them."

"It's sad," I said. Mom and I said nothing for a long time.

Then she said, "You'll want to take a good, hot bath when we get home," she said. "I've got some ice melting. We get it from ponds inland. We live right by the sea, but we can't use sea ice. Too salty."

"Do the people on the coast like you?" I asked.

"The kids like to come to school. It gives them something to do."

"I don't think they like me as much as I like them," I said.

"Well, you have to realize, honey, that we come from such extreme cultures. For a long time now, people have come and brought changes. Surviving in this harsh environment once gave their lives meaning. Now they can order food and clothing through the mail every time they get their government checks. Why should men hunt or trap? Why should women scrape hides or sew skins? We can't blame them if they don't like us very much. We're intruders. We don't belong here."

Below us, ponds shone like silver dollars. The trees became sparse, then disappeared altogether. The world became whiter and bleaker. Snow squalls obscured our view.

"Will we ever go home again?" I asked.

"Most of the time I was married to your father I wanted to go home, but I was already there. Home is more of a feeling than a place."

After that, she said nothing more.

We landed by the sea. People were there to meet us. It was a windy beachfront village with geometric walls of ice along the shoreline. Bundled villagers took my duffel bag and bedroll and helped me onto a sled behind a snowmobile. The wind was so strong we were leaning sideways.

"Allison?"

"Allison? Allison?"

I could hear my name in the wind.

Mom pulled her woolen scarf across her face. "They've heard all about you from me," she said.

Several people climbed into the sled with us. A man straddled the snowmobile, gunning the engine. Within minutes, we were in front of a low, rectangular building.

I followed Mom up the icy, sloping steps. She struck the latch with her arm to loosen it. The metal was too cold to touch even with mittens on. Then she yanked open the heavy outer door.

A crowd of people followed, their faces covered with wool, their ruffs blowing in the wind, their brown eyes staring. People in Sikik's village had looked at me the same way. I smiled.

"You can visit tomorrow," Mom said. "I think we need some time to ourselves, don't you?" She shut the outer door and flicked on a wall switch. The entrance was flooded with light. "Ah, the generator's working."

She unlocked an inner door and we entered the living quarters. An oil stove stood in the center of the room. There was an old, lopsided sofa, a couple of straight-backed chairs, a rickety table, and some shelves loaded with Mom's books. There was even a lamp for reading.

The things Johnny Skye had left behind were there. My horses had been set up on a shelf in a tiny room.

"One of the pilots brought your stuff out long ago," Mom said. "You can arrange things any way you like."

There was a framed picture of Dad and the picture of Mom and me outside our house in Huntington Beach.

"Welcome home, Allison," Mom said. "Such as it is!"

"It's fine, Mom, just fine," I said.

She dipped water from a plastic barrel and heated it on the stove. She made me a bubble bath in a big aluminum tub that she set up in my room. She gave me a towel and a bottle of shampoo. I sank gratefully into the hot water and closed my eyes. If I had a million wishes, I couldn't have wanted anything more.

"I get case lots from Anchorage," she said. "I've got about forty-eight cans of peaches, lots of mushrooms, soups, almost anything you can get canned. No fresh fruit or vegetables, though."

"I'd love a good cheeseburger," I said. "Or pizza."

She laughed. "So would I," she said. "What's your next choice?"

"Spaghetti?"

"That I can do."

I stayed in the tub until the water was cold. Then I pulled on my old, familiar furry slippers and a pair of gray sweats.

We sat at a dilapidated table in the smallest kitchen in the world and ate canned spaghetti. It tasted delicious.

"I must stay until breakup no matter how tough it gets. I promised. I signed a contract."

"And after that?" I asked.

"After that, I don't know," she said. She looked down at her plate but didn't pick up her fork. "*You* didn't sign any contract, though. If you want to go back, I can make arrangements."

"Go back?" I said.

"Yes, to Dana Point, to Dad."

"But I only just got here," I said.

She laughed. "You mean you want to stay after all you've been through?"

"Especially after that," I said.

"Our being here won't make a great deal of difference, not in the long run, not to the Iñupiat people," she said.

After all the years of being her daughter, I finally understood Mom. She'd come to Alaska thinking she could change things, but the Arctic had changed her.

"All I need is just one child who needs me, one child who really wants to learn and deserves the chance," she said. "That would make it seem worthwhile."

"What about Oolik?" I asked.

"You mean the girl by the river?"

"She *really* wants to go to school," I said.

"Oh, I don't know, honey. That's a big responsibility. She'd have to leave her home."

"She could stay with us. There's plenty of room." Mom dipped a fork into the canned spaghetti as she thought about it. I knew how Mom's mind worked. She was already thinking up special projects.

Mom looked up, an eyebrow raised. "Do you think she'd come all the way to the coast?"

"Why not?" I nodded. "It might make a difference."

We grinned at each other.

"Allison, honey, they saved your life," she said. "I'll be forever grateful to them for that. I want to give them something for taking care of you."

But what could she give them?

They had oil for their stoves, moose to eat, and places to sleep. I thought of Ikayauq's well-trained dogs and Matu's fine mukluks. I pictured Sikik in her warm hut, sewing skins, and talking with friends. I remembered Oolik's new baby brother.

"I can't think of anything they need," I said. "Not a single thing."